UNDERDOG

NOVELS BY MICHAEL Z. LEWIN

Underdog
Called By a Panther
And Baby Will Fall
Late Payments
Out of Season
Hard Line
Missing Woman
Outside In
The Silent Salesman
Night Cover
The Enemies Within
The Way We Die Now
Ask the Right Question

UNDERDOG

MICHAEL Z. LEWIN

THE MYSTERIOUS PRESS

Published by Warner Books

A Time Warner Company

Mysterious Press books are published by Warner Books, Inc., 1271 Avenue of the Americas, New York, NY 10020.

A Time Warner Company

Printed in the United States of America

First printing: November 1993

10 9 8 7 6 5 4 3 2 1

Library of Congress Cataloging-in-Publication Data

Lewin, Michael Z.
Underdog / Michael Z. Lewin.
p. cm.
ISBN 0-89296-440-5
I. Title.
PS3562.E929U5 1993
813´.54--dc20 92-59959
CIP

For Helen Wingfield

Who read James Whitcomb Riley in class,
to me and other Hoosier writers.

ACKNOWLEDGMENTS

One of the starting points for this novel was the importance of stories for getting through life. Jan Moro's needs in this respect are extreme. Jan needs to hear and tell stories to function and I needed stories to write about Jan. These came from many places and times. They came via memory from my father, mother, sister and Uncle Don. They came via airmail from tapes of Garrison Keillor, recorded from the radio and sent three thousand miles. They came via airwaves closer to home. And they came as viators from friends: Sheryl Turk, Dick Linsley, Kate Butler, Liza Cody, and Alice Schloss and her many friends. As it happens, my own need for stories is pretty extreme too.

MZL
March 1993
Somerset

UNDERDOG

1.

When I woke up I was cold clear through. That made me hopping mad, for letting myself get into that condition, which is not a comfortable one.

Usually I keep a good eye on how cold or hot it's getting and I plan accordingly. This was October and it was that first night with sharp coldness in it, the coldness that tells you to get set for winter. But I had been so distracted by the excitement of the evening that when I bedded down under a railroad bridge I didn't even bother to unroll my sleeping bag I was so preoccupied. The result was the cold hit me harder than a kick from behind.

Cold is *not* a good thing to let yourself suffer from and I knew right away I was going to have to do something about it, no matter what it cost. So, I got all my things together and I crawled out to the road. I walked fast to where I could dig up some money and then I went to a restaurant and spent it, every bit. I bought an extra-big breakfast and I drank lots and lots of coffee.

After a time I finally began to feel my toes, and that's when I knew it was all right to start thinking about my plans again, though the very first plan had to be to open up the place I use in the winter, even though Rosie was just about due back from her sister trip. I didn't need to worry about the cold with Rosie around, but she wasn't, so I did.

At least I wasn't wet. It can take days to get warm again if I'm wet too. I got thrown into Pogues Run once, one of those wrong place at the wrong time situations. That was the very devil for getting warm again, even though it was in springtime.

But I can swim which made me better off than one guy I knew that got thrown into a river for fun and he drowned. The guys that did it just walked away and probably didn't even know what they'd done. When someone in a bar told me what happened to young Ryan it screwed up my head for days, it was so sad. A kid, only just out of confinement and beginning to find his way. Then something like *that* happens. It makes me mad and sad to think about it even now.

After I drank about as much coffee as I could squeeze in I went to the men's room and I spent a long time in there too. It's easy to neglect your hygiene, especially when you're thinking about discomfort, but I make it a rule to keep presentable and I work hard at it, like keeping my nails clean, and not leaving scuffs on my shoes. I truly believe being presentable is of vital importance if you're a small businessman.

It's also important so's you're not confused with the homeless riffraff there is around. Not that I've got anything against most of them. Some days I spend a lot of time talking to them and I give them good tips. But I still wonder why they don't make more of their lives. If I can pull myself together, so can they.

And I'm *not* homeless. What I am is by way of being a

small businessman who chooses not to be lumbered with one particular business or one particular premises with all that heartache and tax and rent. I like to keep my options open. I like to keep a positive attitude to the opportunity of new things, which I believe is another key to being a success. If you're all tied up one particular place, you've got no chance to stretch out and grab if something better comes along.

Once I was warm and clean I headed north, which I know is not everybody's idea of a winter direction. But this was just to the Fairgrounds, which is where they have the State Fair in the summer but which is mostly quiet and locked up in the winter. I have a place there that I use when Rosie's away and if I don't have important business somewhere else in town.

It's a good place because I can sleep and stay warm in it without anybody bothering me. What I do is go to the corner of the Fairgrounds fence where the Monon Railroad used to meet the street across from the Deaf School. The Monon is long gone now but there are big bushes growing against the fence near a gate that leads in from the street. Each year I cut a hole in the fence where the bushes hide it and nobody fixes the hole again until coming up time for the State Fair. I've had my easy way in and out through the fence three straight winters now.

In fact, nowadays I even have a pair of wire cutters that I keep special for the fence-cutting job. I found them two years ago in a box by a garbage can on the street.

It's purely amazing what people throw away. I saw a private detective say the same thing on TV in a bar one time, but he meant letters and bills that could help him prove divorces and frauds. What I look for is clothes to wear and stuff to resell and there's never any shortage in the long run. Whenever I need cash I know I can find money waiting to be picked up and sold. It's just sitting there on the streets, especially if you learn the days people put things out.

I get a lot of my clothes that way, like my Pringle sweater though of course I don't wear that all the time. In the winter what I do is carry it in my plastic accordion file, which is where I carry most of my necessary things apart from my sleeping bag.

The wire cutters don't go in the file because I use them only once a year and at the one place. Them I wrap tight in a plastic bag and I bury them under the bushes by the Fairgrounds fence so they're right on the spot. I keep a lot of things buried in handy places around town and I keep the places in my head.

I learned about the Fairgrounds in the first place because I met this guy in a bar who puts together clean-up crews for after special city events. So I was on a crew for after the State Fair and that's how come I know my way around at the Fairgrounds. What the guy pays isn't much but it's in cash and you also get to take away any of the trash that you want. When you're on "cash and trash" it pays to keep your eyes open.

The crew I like best, though, is the one for the 500 Mile Race and for the weekends of the time trials before it. What I like is not the trash but that I can stop sometimes and stand by the fences and listen to the engines of the race cars as they go by. That's music to me. That's poetry. They rhyme, the Indy cars.

"You get off on those engines," Rosie said to me once. And it's true. I do. It's true/I do. Another thing I am is a natural songwriter and I've got a plan for that too, when I get a chance. I'm going to start with a public access TV show.

Rosie doesn't really understand though. She said to me once, "Why don't you ever go out to Weir Cook if you like big engines so much?" But that's something completely different. Weir Cook's an airport and airplanes are just airplanes, but out at the track, those are *cars*.

A lot of people came up to Indy from someplace further south. Not me. I came down from Detroit, which was my base for a long time, though I traveled around a lot, even to Canada and Mexico. But a few years ago, when I got out, I decided I better leave all that.

And, O.K., I'm also a small businessman in the way of not being a tall businessman. And that's why I'm in Indy again at all because when I set out from Detroit my idea was to be a jockey. I thought I'd go to Kentucky and ride horses. This guy I shared with for a while was from Louisville and he kept telling me how they're crying out for guys my size who are as strong as me. But I never made it to Kentucky. My money ran out when I got to Indy, which was about five years ago. Then once I got off the bus here I said, "Hey, why not?"

In fact, I was a kid in Indy for six years before a certain incident when I was thirteen. I used to think Indy would be a bad town to come back to, but when I fetched up at the bus station I realized the town had changed and so had I. It was nearly twenty years. Who remembers? And there's something to be said for a town where you aren't a complete stranger to it.

And, like everybody else who's ever been here, Indy was someplace I was hankering to come back to, in my heart.

My first year at the Fairgrounds I tried a few different places, but the one I use now and like best is a guard's hut near the gate out to the street. It's only little, but it's easier to feel warm in the hut than in the bigger places further along the road that leads to the inside of the Fairgrounds.

What I do is after I cut the hole in the fence there's this window I break. I've done the same three years in a row now. I break the window to get in the hut and then I block the pane up and lay my sleeping bag out and I'm warm free.

The first year I fixed the window with cardboard, but now I have a piece of clear plastic, almost the exact right size, and I bury that along with the wire cutters. I wedge the piece of plastic in the frame and it looks just about like glass.

Come the morning I leave by the door, like a normal citizen. The lock's a Yale and all I have to do is click it so's the tongue stays swallowed and bingo, I come and go as I please, whenever I don't have business elsewhere in town. I leave the door unlocked like that all winter long and I've never had the trouble of someone else using it.

If I go from the Fairgrounds to downtown it takes me

about an hour if I walk direct, though usually I don't because there are a lot of places to stop on the way. Could be places for collecting, or places to talk to contacts, or even the laundromat.

In fact, the idea that made me so excited that I let myself get cold had to do with the laundromat, in a way. The idea was for a slow-release deodorant—like the slow-release pills they've got for headaches. Only this slow-release deodorant doesn't get put on the person, it goes straight on the clothes. That way the person can get nervous and sweaty, but the clothes still smell sweet and the person can wear them for as long as he or she likes. I still think it's an idea with good potential. Another thing about it is that it's greener than putting chemical deodorant straight on the person, because that stuff tampers with what the body does naturally. It was an idea that came to me during a heat wave in August. I figured if I could tell the right entrepreneur about the slow-release deodorant for clothes then I had me a real winner and a business success.

What got me so excited was that I got a fresh idea about who the entrepreneur could be.

2.

In the day before the night I got cold I did some good finding and selling business, so come evening I stopped at a place called Sam's Saloon. There were half a dozen guys at the bar and three more in suits at a table. At the bar they were all shooting the breeze about the mayor election, which was a pretty hot topic.

But then one of the suit guys at the table, he suddenly stood up and said, real loud, "Do you fuckers *have* to talk about goddamn politics?"

Well, that stopped the whole place, and the guy said, "I get politics at home till it comes out of my fucking ears. I get aborted babies. I get whether chiropractors ought to take fucking blood samples. I get what shade of green this candidate or that is. So, today on my way home I stop in here for a relaxing drink and what do I get? Politics! I am sick to fucking death of politics."

The bartender started to say something about how this guy should go someplace else if he didn't like the company, but the suit guy raised his hands and said, "I know I'm out of line. I know. I run a place myself. But all I want to say was, if you guys'll talk about something else, I'll buy a drink for everybody in the joint."

Well, it went quiet at that while everybody at the bar took a look at everybody else. And suddenly, instead of thinking this guy in his suit was a jerk, suddenly everybody thought he was a pal and we'd talk about anything he wanted, thanks very much.

I was only nursing a beer, like I do, but I ordered a boilermaker and a lot of the others did the same and the guy in the suit didn't bat an eyelid. He just nodded to one of his friends, and that guy got up and paid with a hundred dollar bill.

Then it went quiet, because there was a problem what to talk about instead of the mayor election. The quiet wasn't comfortable, so I decided to break the ice. I told a story I'd heard the day before in another bar.

It was about how one time there was this guy who took his dog to the movies, right in, and sat the dog down in the next seat, and the movie was one called *War and Peace.*

Anyhow, the dog sat up in the seat and kept awake, and it wasn't long before the people near to him began to realize that this dog was paying attention to the screen. And the people realized that the dog seemed to understand everything and to be having a good time. It nodded when something good happened, and growled when there was something bad, and it even wagged its tail at the jokes and whimpered when things were sad, all like the things the people nearby were feeling.

Well, this went on through the whole movie and when it was over, a big crowd gathered around the man and his dog and everybody said, "That's amazing."

"What's amazing?" the guy asked.

"Your dog," the people said. "Your dog wagged his tail at the jokes and growled at the danger and he really seemed to enjoy the movie."

"Yeah, he did enjoy it, didn't he?" the man said. "And I agree, that is amazing. Because he didn't like the book at all."

Well, everybody else laughed and banged their fists on the bar, but the drinks guy put his hands over his face.

I asked if something was wrong.

"Can we skip the stories about fucking animals? All right? Because if it isn't politics, the other thing I get nonstop is my old lady talking about the 'terrible' things people do to goddamn animals."

Well, that shut me up and I was going to ask if there were other things we weren't supposed to talk about and whether maybe that was worth another drink, but a guy next to me asked, "If you get all that aggravation, man, why you stay with the bitch?"

"Don't get me wrong," the suit guy said. "She's a hell of a woman, my wife. And I owe her a lot. I owe her just about everything, to tell you the truth. But once she gets a bur up her butt that woman sure does talk."

The guy that asked nodded in sympathy and then a kid the other end from me asked if it was O.K. to tell a Lone Ranger story.

"Sure," the drinks guy said.

So the kid told this old story about the Lone Ranger where the Lone Ranger is tied up at the stake and he whispers to Tonto and Tonto keeps bringing him women but the Lone Ranger finally gets mad and shouts, "No, dammit! I said, 'Bring a *posse*!' "

And that set everybody off for about half an hour.

Finally the guy who bought the drinks looked at his watch and stood up and said, "Well thanks, fellas. I really appreciate it, but it's time for me to go face some mouth music."

Everybody began to say "Thanks again," but the guy said, "But first I got a story now for you, one I heard in the navy."

So we all turned around to face him.

He said, "There was an Italian, a Nigger, a Jew and a

Greek." He looked around the room. "Is there anybody else here I can offend?" And that got a laugh by itself. So he said, "This Italian, Nigger, Jew and Greek all got killed, and went to Heaven. But at the gate they found out that them going to Heaven was a big fucking mistake. Well, Saint Peter went inside and had a little confab with the Big G and then Saint Peter came back and said to the four guys, 'We've decided to send you back for a while, on trial. But if you really want to get into Heaven instead of going to Hell, each of you is going to have to give up what he likes best. If you don't give it up, then poof, you're history. Down you go to Hell.' Well, suddenly the four guys are back on earth and they're walking along the street together. And then, this girl walks by and the Italian says, 'Hey! Look at those tits!' And poof, the Italian was gone. Well, the Nigger and the Jew and the Greek walk a little further down the street and they come to a guy selling fruit off a truck and the Nigger says, 'Look guys, watermelon!' And poof, the Nigger is gone. So that leaves the Jew and the Greek and they're walking along and the Jew sees a quarter on the sidewalk and he bends down to pick it up. And poof, the Greek is gone."

There was a moment that we were quiet working it out, but then everybody started laughing.

Even though it wasn't the kind of story that I like, I laughed along too, and the suit guy said, "Ha, surprised you with that one," and he left with all of us at the bar whistling and stomping, till he got out the door.

Then I said, "I don't get it. What was the joke?"

The bartender said, "When the Jew bends down we're supposed to think it's him that's going to Hell because of the quarter, but instead it's the Greek because the Jew's showing him his behind."

"I see, I see," I said. "I just didn't know that Greeks were supposed to be like that."

"We're not," the young guy down the bar from me said.

That got a laugh too.

And the young guy said, "Fella's just a fuckin' asshole," meaning the suit guy, and that got a bigger laugh yet.

Then an old man next to me said, "You know who that was, don't you?"

"Was that somebody?" I said.

"That was Billy Cigar," the old man said.

"*That* was Billy Cigar?" I said, and I looked at the door. "Wow!" And I began to get excited.

I'd heard of Billy Cigar, but I'd never met him before. In fact, Cigar isn't his right name, but that's how everybody knows him because it sounds like his real name which is Sigra.

People know about Billy Cigar because he pulled off this enormous score somewhere down in South America. He went in there with his wife and a team and they all came out with millions of bucks. That's what they say. For sure, enough money that he could come to Indy and buy a club. The reason he came to Indy was Indy is where Billy Sigra grew up and his mother still lives here. The club is the Linger Longer Lounge and he gets music acts in there most Friday and Saturday nights.

The wife, which must have been the same one he was complaining about, came originally from the country they hit in South America. And it's her that had the great idea for the whole thing which is why he made the speech about how he owed his wife everything.

The great thing about her idea wasn't how much it was for, or because it was easy, because it wasn't. It took a helicopter, which Billy learned how to fly in the navy in Vietnam, and they had to kill people, which I suppose he learned over there too. Nobody knows exactly how many. One guy in the bar said he'd heard five and another guy heard twenty. But however many it really was, there was an awful stink about it for a while, on the TV news and everything, because the people down in the country in South America wanted Billy and his wife sent back real bad.

But the great thing about the idea was that the country was

one of the kind that doesn't do extraditions with America. That made it a lot easier for Billy to fight off the country's legal tries to get him sent back.

One guy in Sam's said he'd been where Billy told a whole bar about the robbery and how all he's got to do for the rest of his life is fight off the temptation to go for a vacation in South America. That's some joke.

You hear about guys who rob banks in this country and then run off to Cuba or someplace. But who wants to live somewhere foreign, even with enough money to buy everything you could want? It's O.K. for some guys, but a normal guy, eventually he's going to start missing things.

I met a guy in a bar once who came back from hiding in a foreign country after six years, and it was because he missed creamed corn—the kind in cans. He said he kept dreaming about the taste, which is not my own taste, but I know what he means.

That guy was unusual, because usually guys come back for family or because they're sick or something. When I met this guy, he'd been back a year, and so far so good. But mostly the cops and the FBI remember and catch guys, so it's a real problem, even if you can pull something big enough and get away with it.

But doing it the other way around, so you escape by coming home, that's brilliant! If I had had that idea in the first place, I could have sold it for money. But I didn't have it. Who had the great extradition idea was Linda Cigar, Billy's missus. She thought it up because she came from the country and because there was this guy down there she knew all about, and how he kept money and jewels and gold in his own house.

Linda is Billy's second wife, the one he's got now. There was a story about the first wife, but that was in San Diego where Billy was before moving back home to Indy. There was a ruckus about the first wife and another guy and it ended with Billy resigning from the police force before he got fired.

That's the other thing. For about ten years after the navy, until he met Linda, Billy Cigar was a cop.

The way it worked out, meeting Billy Cigar was what made me get so cold. This was because later that night I suddenly remembered my clothes deodorant idea from the summer and I got it in mind that Billy Cigar might be just the entrepreneur to try the deodorant idea on. And while I was thinking how to go about that I didn't think about the weather, and that's why I let myself get cold. So the next day of the cold snap I set myself up in the guard's hut at the Fairgrounds so I could think about whatever I wanted without any trouble.

3.

As soon as I woke up after that first night in the guard's hut I knew something was different. What happened was this truck came in. It was the creaking sound as the gate swung open that woke me up. I was out of my sleeping bag and watching before the guy closed the gate behind him. There'd never been a truck come through the gate before, not in three winters I've been sleeping out there.

So, I walked along after the truck to see where it went. If suddenly they were going to start using the Deaf School side of the Fairgrounds in the winter I wanted to know. I like to sleep out of the way, of course, but it also could mean stuff might come up, opportunities.

The truck itself was like an old pickup Daddy used to drive on the farm, bigger than a street pickup and with a tarp tied over whatever was on the back. Where it went was a warehouse building not far down the road. During the fair they keep sweeping machines and straw bales and some secretaries in there. The machines and straw are in this big room and the secretaries use a couple of offices attached on the side.

I knew all about the building from being on the cleanup crew. I even slept in one of the offices a couple of times the first winter. I got a buzz out of that because the window frames had polished wood sills and the doors were thick. But I wasn't comfortable from the noise. There are rats in that building. So I tried the guard's hut and the rest is history.

This kid I knew in Lafayette told me a story about rats one time, about eating them and how their tails are good roasted crisp and dipped in ketchup. He said the rest of a rat you might as well throw away. I never believed him, but I remember him telling me like it was yesterday. I was near enough sixteen and we were hiding in a barn, 'cause we'd run away, and it was our first night and we heard these sounds. Jeff was about as city a boy as there could be but he swore it was rats and he told me that story. I asked him how he knew and he said it was because his grandad told him.

In Detroit later on I met the old man, but he was demented so I never asked him about the rats. But Jeff's uncle said the old man used to be a cook, so maybe it was true. It was Jeff that got me to Detroit and his uncle that got me into traveling and all that trouble but I've never been hard enough up to try out what Jeff said about rats' tails that night in the barn.

Next to where the truck was parked there were a couple of trees and I came around to look at it from that side. I don't have much trouble about people noticing me, but if there's some cover one way and none the other, what's the point of taking chances?

The wind was blowing my direction and even before I got close to the truck I heard this eerie moaning and it was wild and sad. I stopped to try to figure out what it was.

For a minute I thought it was people screwing under the

tarp on the back of the truck, because the sound was something like that. Only this sound wasn't happy and it went on and on and on and I couldn't think how anybody would need to be at it on the back of a pickup so early in the morning, but maybe I'm just not romantic enough.

The more I listened, though, the more voices I heard, not just one or two. So I worked my way up closer.

When I got to the truck I heard it wasn't moans at all, not like people make. It was dog sounds. But not howls like at the moon or when the radio's on or someone's screaming, but sad sounds like the dog's master was dead and it'd given up on living.

At the back of the truck I loosened the tarp and there they were, about eight of them, and as soon as they saw the light they stopped moaning and started jumping around in their cages and being excited. Only instead of full-grown dogs they looked soft and lively like puppies, except they were so big. Puppies of some big kind of dog. Each one was in a wire cage just about hardly big enough for it.

And then, this guy grabbed me by the arm.

I nearly jumped out of my shoes.

"What the f-f-fuck you doing?" he said.

"Just looking. Hi. My name's Jan."

He was a thin guy in a gray jacket and his face looked gray too, hollow around the cheeks, only he had a black eye and a swollen nose and he was maybe twenty. He was a lot bigger than me, but then most people are.

I said, "I was going to go in and ask for a job, but I thought I better see what business you were in first."

He looked hard at me. Then he pulled at me and started walking me to the warehouse and he never once loosened up on his grip.

We went through the door to the office part of the building. Whoever was using the place, they had put in a table and chairs and a refrigerator and a microwave and a phone. But I heard barks and other sounds from where I couldn't see, so I guessed it was some kind of a dog business that they had rented the whole building for and not just a social call made by the truck driver.

There were three guys in the next room and from as soon as I got marched in I could tell who was in charge. He was built like a brick outhouse and he had a face that looked like streaky clay scooped up from the hole. The guy had star quality, he really did. "What you got there, Warren?" he asked my gray guy with the black eye.

"He was l-l-looking in my t-t-truck, Mr. Cobb. I w-w-watched him. He c-c-come to it slow and s-s-stuck his head in."

The outhouse guy had a longer look at me. "Who are you, shorty?"

It was a chance to pull away from Warren and I did. "Hi," I said. I stuck out my hand. "Name's Jan. I was looking for a job."

"A job?" Cobb said. It was like he had never heard the word before.

Warren said, "That's w-w-what he told me too."

One of the other two guys leaned in and whispered something in Cobb's ear. This guy wore jeans and a flannel shirt. He was big, but not like Cobb, who looked like a lineman. The whispering guy was in his fifties and bald, but he had a close-cut beard that was brown and gray mixed and all in all what he looked was pure meanness.

It was a long whisper but it ended with Cobb saying, "That's good," and the mean-looking one turned to the last guy. "Al," he said, and nodded in my direction.

Al came over to me. He was big too, but he was the only one that looked like he had any softness to him at all, because his face wasn't set hard in a frown. "Lie on the floor," he said.

"Sure. Whatever you want."

The guy patted me down all the way and emptied my pockets. That was easy though. Wasn't nothing in them.

Cobb said, "Now what kind of guy goes around with empty pockets?"

I rolled up to my knees. "A guy looking for work who'll do just about anything and who knows how to keep his mouth shut."

Cobb thought about that.

The mean-looking one said, "He's too fucking little."

"But I'm strong as hell," I said.

Al said, "Pin a curly tail on him and we could use him for training."

Cobb and the mean-looking one with the beard laughed at that. Warren didn't though, and I didn't know what they were talking about. I didn't like the sound of it much.

Cobb said. "Pete, take him in the back. I'll talk to him after we get the dogs settled in."

"Tie him up?"

Cobb laughed. "I'm going to talk to him, not fuck him, Pete. You always want to tie everybody up. You got a thing about rope?"

Warren laughed with Cobb and Al this time, but Pete didn't laugh. He just looked mean. "Come on, shorty," he said.

He pointed to a door. I went through it and there was a passage with another door at the end. He pushed me along and that was the john, which had a sink and a chair. There was also a window.

I thought Pete was just going to leave me, but he came in and closed the door behind us. And that's when I really got scared.

"Sit down," he said.

I moved to the chair, but he said, "On the can." He sat on the chair. Then he took off one of his shoes.

"Hey," I said. "What you doing?"

He looked at me, one of the meanest looks I've ever seen. I was sweating bullets by now because sure as shooting I was the dog around here and he was the cage.

Then he took off his sock.

"Look, pal," I began. I was going to try to get him talking. That's what they say to do.

But he didn't go for it. He stopped me. "*You* look."

"What at?"

"My fucking foot."

I looked at his foot. It only had two toes.

"Nice," I said.

"I got hungry one day. I had to eat the other three toes."

I looked at the foot again.

"Ever since then, I haven't felt I was a whole man. You get me?"

"No. I don't."

"Sometimes I think to myself, 'Pete,' I think, 'you ought to get yourself some new toes off somebody.' That's what I think. And you know what?"

"What?"

"I think that somebody could be you."

"Me?"

He put his sock back on.

He said, "I'm going to go unload the truck now."

"Yeah?"

He put his shoe back on. He double-knotted the lace so it wouldn't come untied. I do that too. He said, "If you're still in this room after the truck is unloaded, I'm going to come back in here and take off three of your toes and nobody will ever find the rest of you. Do I make myself clear?"

I nodded.

"For your sake, little man, I hope so." He got up and went out the door and locked it.

4.

I hardly had my breath back from being scared before I was up trying the window. I was afraid I wouldn't be able to open it and that I'd have to break the frame and they'd hear the glass fall out. But the window gave as soon as I put some muscle into it and it was big enough for me to slip through easily.

The john side of the warehouse wasn't where the truck was, so I got back to the guard's hut without any of them seeing me. I picked up my sleeping bag, money and the accordion file I carry with everything important in it, and I hightailed it towards town.

There are different theories about your important things. Some guys say you're better off having everything you own with you all the time. Others say you should hide stuff in case you get rousted. Me, I'm a hider, since I got done in St. Louis one time.

I was on a bus on the way to Detroit and all I was doing in St. Louis was laying over for an hour while they cleaned the bus up. It was the same bus all the way from the Mexico border.

I took my bags and sat in the station. In fact I like sitting in bus stations, because you see interesting things, but that day I wasn't paying attention because sitting there was like still being in the bus, in my mind. Suddenly these two guys came and stood either side of me and grabbed my arms and said, "Come on, quick!" and marched me off to a white marble wall in the hallway outside the men's room.

I kept asking what they thought they were doing, but one of them said, "Police," and waved this badge in my face so I went along until they stopped.

Then the guy said, "Show me your ID."

I explained about the bus.

"Let's see the ticket," the other one said.

I held up the ticket, and I opened my wallet to a driver's license I had, though, as it happened, it was not one in my own name. The second guy said, "Let me look," and took them. Then the first one made me kneel with my face to the wall and my hands behind my head.

The one with my stuff said, "My advice, little fella, is be careful. Lot of strange people in this town."

"Oh yeah?" I said, but he didn't say anything back. "Can I get up now?"

But nobody answered.

"Hey, can I get up?" I looked around. All I saw was an old man with a cane trying to figure out what I was doing kneeling with my face to the wall and talking to myself. The two guys were gone. And, of course, so were my bags when I got back to where I was sitting. That did not go down well in Detroit and they never sent me on that kind of trip again.

I've got hidey-holes all around town. If I ever decide to move somewhere else it'll take me most of a week to gather everything up. Most of the places have some money in them, which is a way to make sure I don't get caught without cash. Mostly I hide quarters because a little wet doesn't hurt change.

Around town there's lots of stuff besides money. Some is useful, like the wire cutters, and some I'm saving in case it might be valuable or good for something one day. I've even got a gun and three bullets wrapped in plastic bags. I have never fired a gun in my life, but this one I won from a guy I was playing cards with.

I was on the south side and he was the uncle—well, he said he was the uncle—of a woman who let me stay in her house for a month while Rosie was on a sister trip. It was gin rummy and neither of us was very good but one of us stayed off the gin so I won about thirty bucks and then Uncle lost another hand and said he couldn't pay. I didn't care because he was a nice guy, but when I said it he suddenly got mean and said no one ever said that he didn't pay his debts and he took out this gun.

I had an uncomfortable moment, especially when he pulled the trigger. But it wasn't loaded and he said it was worth everything he had lost to me that night and more, so what happened was he made me buy it off him with the money he just lost. And he threw in the bullets.

It's like a lot of things, the gun. I figured it might come in handy or be worth something someday. I knew a night watchman one time who used a .22 target pistol to shoot rats till he didn't pay enough attention to what was behind the rat and he put a hole in a tank and flooded the place with cherry syrup. He had to say he shot at a vandal and he ended up a hero, or so he said. He was trying to sell the pistol in a bar.

My gun is a .38 and I'd sell it to a night watchman or a guard. But I wouldn't sell it to someone I thought was going to use it on people. That's a principle I have, and not just because I'd be fingered in a minute as the supplier by a guy in trouble with the police. A self-employed solo businessman has no counterweight at all with bad guys, and the problem is that just about anybody who'll buy a gun in a bar is likely to be up to no good, no matter how much he says it's so his wife can feel safe by her bed.

So I hid the gun to think about it and to see what came up. I hid it near the City-County Building which is where the cops and the courts are in Indy. On the south side they have an area with trees and bushes planted in raised beds. I buried it about a foot down in one of them.

I thought it was funny the night I did it, burying a gun on the same block as cop headquarters.

This morning in October was one day I walked straight downtown without stopping, because I had never got mixed up with a guy that ate his own toes before. In fact I was walking so hard and thinking about it so hard that I went straight through downtown and out the other side.

I only stopped and calmed down when I got hungry. By then I was near a place on Virginia Avenue called Bud's Dugout. Why they call it a "dugout" I don't know, because it's got nothing to do with baseball. It's the bottom floor of a three-floor brick building, and inside it's just a diner with wood tables and a pinball machine and an old woman that runs the place, with the help of a young guy who is the cook.

I eat breakfast there when my schedule has me on the near south side of town. What I like is that the food the old woman serves is cooked how food used to be and she—or the cook—makes it all there and not out of catering packs. And it *isn't* expensive because of that, as if it's cute to have hamburger in a hamburger. Also, in Bud's nobody looks twice at a guy coming in. Even a guy carrying a sleeping bag.

Breakfast is the one meal I like to buy, because I like eggs and sausages and hot toast in the morning and that's about the one thing you will never find in the alley behind a place. Almost anything else though. I've even had filet mignon that was still warm.

Bud's may have kept how it used to be, but most of the Fountain Square area you can't walk around and browse the way you could even five years ago. It's coming to be a rehabilitated part of town with antique stores and fifty dollar restaurants. I guess the old woman feels the pinch of the economy because now she rents out the upstairs to a business with a neon sign and she never used to do that, so it can't be easy for her.

This morning the old woman was working alone, because it was after the rush and there were only two guys left eating. After I ordered I went around the tables and picked up the dirty dishes and brought them over to the counter. I'm in business myself, and I know how it can feel to have more to do than you've got time for.

She smiled and said, "Thanks, young fella," and it suddenly reminded me of another old woman who helped me a lot when I was in a children's home in Lafayette, even though she didn't know that's what she was doing.

I was put in this home when my family broke up after the trial when I was thirteen, and Cissy and Wayne got taken in by relations but I didn't. The home was not a happy day for me. It was so bad that when I got sent to school, I hated it and couldn't talk, not a word, that's how bad it was. There hasn't been another time in my whole life when I couldn't talk.

Anyhow, when the old woman in Bud's brought my food we got to passing the time of day. She's got a nice way of looking at life, that old woman. You can tell she's seen a thing or two. And like me, she looks for the good that comes out of things. For instance, she told me how her son was in trouble with the police, though he was out on bail now, and maybe I'd read about it.

I said I hadn't, but the point is she didn't go on to talk about her son's trouble—which I might have seen on TV in a bar and known about after all. What she said was that the trouble meant that the boy's daughter, the old woman's granddaughter, had moved back to town. "She's been a restless little soul in her life, with a lot of emotion," the old woman said, "but she sees the good side in her father and I think being here for him is good for herself too. It gives her some quiet time to work things out."

"There's a lot to be said for peace and quiet," I said, thinking about the morning I'd had. "And for time to think out what's important to you."

"The little gal even helps me out in the diner, lunchtimes," the old woman said. " 'Course, that could have something to do with her having taken a shine to my cook."

My own daddy used to say, "Everything is good for something," leastwise he said that before some of his own troubles. And I'm sure that the old woman at Bud's would have agreed to that, though I didn't think to say it to her until I was already finished with breakfast and out walking again.

"Everything is good for something," is one of my own philosophies too, even if Daddy doesn't say it anymore, at least not last time I went for a visit, which was a few years back. He seemed pretty sour about life that time, which may count towards why I haven't gone again.

Funny thing is, it was about then I stopped blaming him so much. There's a lot he couldn't help. I even began to think maybe it wasn't so much his fault, him bringing Gloria home. There's just some men that go crazy for a woman, so crazy they don't see what the woman is doing to their own children, they're so blind with it. And maybe my daddy was one of those and really could not help himself. That's what I've come to think, even though it was truly hard for a little kid like me that had lost his own mother. To tell the truth, it was harder on me than on either Cissy or Wayne, because Gloria took to them better than she ever took to me. Wayne was always cute, and Cissy got to brush Gloria's hair and I never did, even though I always did it for my own mother.

In a lot of ways I've come to use my daddy's life as a guideline for me in my own life. Not going blind over a woman is one thing. Never killing somebody is another. But he was just a man, for all that. *Is* just a man, unless something's happened to him I haven't heard.

5.

Being on the south side of town instead of the north side meant I had to make a whole new plan for my day. But things like that happen in a life and sometimes the best stuff turns up when you haven't planned for it.

After breakfast, I started by checking the Golden Goat off Prospect. The Goat is a machine that pays you cash for aluminum cans, but this time it was out of order.

There's a secondhand bookstore near Fountain Square too, and I stopped in there to ask the man what books he was buying now. That can change at different times of year, and the only thing specific he said was old high school yearbooks. It's not that I had books to sell, but fall and spring is a good time for people to clear out their houses with garage sales and on the weekend I sometimes pick up whole boxes of books. When that happens, I divide the books up and take them around to different stores on the basis of what the stores buy, though sometimes it's hard to tell by the covers. Selling books is by no means the best business I do, but it's something if other kinds of business are quiet.

Next what I did was work my way back to downtown, not direct but under the interstates and through all the alleys. The best things I found were a folding deck chair that only needed cleaning, a barbecue apron with hearts and bunnies on it and an old clock with a wood case. I took them and some china doodads and plates to a secondhand store, but I didn't get much.

In fact it felt that I spent the whole day walking and not much of it doing business. But it was clear weather and not too hot or cold, and some days are just like that.

While I was walking I thought a lot, which is what I do, including about the dogs in the truck at the Fairgrounds, but I just couldn't work out what angle of business all that could be.

The dogs were going to be unloaded, and I'd heard the barking from other dogs already in there. But there were no signs outside, like there would be for a pet store.

Some people in the country raise up dogs to sell on their farms, which I know because all Momma and Daddy's people were farmers, and they used to talk about things like that when I was little and they weren't mad. I don't think any of them did dogs themselves, but they talked about people who raised up puppies to sell to pet stores and laboratories. In Indy we have plenty of pet stores and also there's Loftus, the international drug company, that maybe uses dogs to give diseases to and cure them of again. And I remember seeing pictures of beagles that used to smoke cigarettes, but the puppies in the truck were too big for beagles and I don't know whether dogs smoke anymore anyhow.

But I'd never heard of a business to grow dogs that was set up inside a city and not out on a farm. And besides, a business to grow dogs would likely end up with puppies instead of starting with them.

So then I thought maybe it was a business to grow dogs up and train them, maybe to be guard dogs or to attack people. The puppies were big, and I recalled that the soft guy, Al, had said,

"Pin a curly tail on him and we could use him for training," and that might fit, though I didn't understand what that about the curly tail meant. Curly tails are pigs and pinning tails is on donkeys.

I thought about it all a lot during the day, but I never got sure I knew what they were doing out there.

The other thing I thought about was that, for certain, two of those guys were truly dangerous guys: Cobb, the guy in charge, and Pete, who ate his own toes. I've met dangerous guys before and these two were the same, what with their whispering and their jokes about tying people up that ask for a job.

But I didn't understand Pete at all. No two ways about it, Pete had intended me to be scared off and run away, so I wouldn't hang around about the job, even though Cobb had said about talking to me later. Maybe if Cobb offered me a job that meant somehow Pete would lose his. It's all I could think of that would be so important as to make a guy take his shoe and sock off.

I figured I was still probably safe enough sleeping in the guard's hut nearby, as long as I wasn't seen by any of them, and that's not usually a problem for me. In fact, if I felt like it, I could watch them some more and maybe work it all out. But since I was already in town, I decided to stay away from the Fairgrounds at least that night.

My original plan about the deodorant for clothes was to wait till Friday to try to talk to Billy Cigar, when there might be music in his club and he'd be in a good mood. The idea had been to come back to town on Thursday, which was when Rosie was probably due back, and then by Friday I'd be set to do some business again.

But with my whole day's plan being changed anyhow, I decided I might as well go around to the Linger Longer even though it was a Wednesday. Billy Cigar might be there anyway and maybe the right thing was to try him on a quiet night.

I'd need to find a good way to raise the deodorant subject because it could be a tricky thing to explain in its best light. I might have to go to the club more than once before the moment was right.

The Linger Longer Lounge wasn't far out of downtown, almost due east but not as far as the women's prison. The club was a big, one-floor brick building with whitewashed stucco out front and a red awning across the sidewalk all the way to the curb. It was on a corner, just across from a small shopping center. Behind the club it had a parking lot and there was an alley, and on the side away from the corner there was a strip of grass separating it from what even outside smelled like a dry cleaners.

I didn't try to go in, because I wasn't ready, but the club looked closed anyway. I went across to the little shopping center. That had a Chinese restaurant in it, and my plan was find somewhere to sit in the shadows out back of that.

But then I got a great new idea, from when I was looking on the door at the front of the restaurant. What triggered me off was a red circle sign with a cigarette and a red line through it that meant people shouldn't smoke inside.

As I walked around back, I got to thinking that people who have to smoke cigarettes must feel picked on nowadays. I see these no smoking circles all over the place. The people I know that smoke mostly don't want to do it but they can't help it, maybe from taking it up when there just wasn't anything else for them to do to pass the time. I know a lot of guys that started cigarettes like that. Then they come out and try to lead a normal life again and all these places around town don't want them. It must be hard.

The great idea I had for them was to put together a hood, sort of like half a mask. A smoker would put the hood on over his nose and mouth and it would be built so that it hung down and was sealed somehow and it would keep all the smoke inside. That way nobody could complain, and the smoker could walk around and go into as many stores and restaurants as he wanted to.

The more I thought about a smoking hood, the better I

liked it. On the streets alone you still see a whole lot of smoking people, and that doesn't count the ones who stay inside. It could either be that an entrepreneur would set it up and corner the market, or maybe one of the cigarette companies would use hoods to fight back all the places that stopped people smoking there.

I like to have great ideas. It makes me feel more worthwhile about the day.

While I was waiting, I got my good shirt out of the accordion file—which is where it keeps pretty flat. If I'd had it with me I'd have worn my Pringle sweater to go to the club, but that was still stored at Rosie's, waiting for her to get back, which was only tomorrow or the next day at the most. She goes on long trips with her sister, Tulip, Rosie does. They can be for months even, but we have the planning worked out so I can be sure to meet her at the bus and carry her bags, which she likes.

Without the sweater it had to be the jacket I wear all day, which is brown corduroy. Before I got dressed, I found something to eat behind the restaurant, though not what I like best at a Chinese, which is egg rolls. But it was while I was eating that I began to think that if I worked it out right, the smoke hood could be an idea to put to Billy Cigar, if for some reason he decided not to like the clothes deodorant. It's always good when you're in business to have a second idea, and if I played things right having this new idea could change my whole life. Not that my life is so bad, but we could all do with some improvement.

I changed shirts and freshed up the jacket with a fabric brush, and I buffed up my shoes and combed my hair. Then I found a dark place to leave my stuff and I went to the front door of the Linger Longer, which was now open and had a guy on the door in a uniform.

"Hi," I said. "The name's Jan." I stuck out my hand.

But he wasn't friendly. He looked down at me and he said, "What's your problem, short-stuff?"

"Is the boss around tonight?"

"What's it to you?"

"I was talking to him day before yesterday and I've got some business I could put his way. Is he around?"

"No."

"Is he going to be in later on?"

"This is Wednesday," the guy said.

Before I could ask him to tell me something I didn't know, he stepped away from me and put on this big smile and held the door for three guys and said, "Evening, Mr. Harris."

One of the guys said, "Evening, Ed," and passed over a tip.

Ed said, "Thank you, thank you, Mr. Harris. Y'all have a good time."

When the door was closed again I said, "Looks like a good job," more by way of trying to be friendly than because I thought it was true.

"I ain't complaining," Ed said.

"So, Mr. Cigar doesn't come in on Wednesdays?"

"Nope," Ed said. "He visits his mother, and even if he did come in, you wouldn't get in to see him dressed like that."

"What's wrong with the way I'm dressed?"

"Ain't got no tie on," Ed said. "You gotta have a tie on."

"But one of the guys with Mr. Harris didn't have a tie on."

"But you ain't with Mr. Harris," Ed said. We looked at each other, but we both knew how the world is. Ed said, "I got my discretion."

"When is Mr. Cigar usually here?"

"Can be any day but Wednesday, and for sure this Saturday because we got a big act in, with a cover charge."

"Thanks," I said. "I'll be seeing you." I waved as I walked away but I didn't give him a tip.

I didn't hang around near the club. What I did was pick up my stuff and change back to my ordinary shirt and head downtown, only I stopped at a bar on the way. In the bar I nursed a beer, like I do, and I listened to the guys telling stories until it was late enough to sleep.

The story I liked best was told by a guy called Jim and it was about how once he was in a bar and as he was about to leave, the bartender asked him to drive a drunk home.

Jim found out that the guy didn't live very far away so, what the hell, he said O.K., he'd do it. But when he got the drunk off his stool, the guy just fell over on the floor. "Lordy me," Jim thinks, but he's said he'll take the guy home, so he gathers him up off the floor and the guy rubberlegs outside to Jim's car and just about gets into the passenger seat.

Jim drives the guy to his street and the guy is conscious enough to point out which house is his and Jim is grateful to get there without the guy spewing up on the upholstery.

Jim parks and goes around to the passenger door and opens it and the guy falls out all over the sidewalk. But Jim gets him up and through the gate and on his porch and rings the bell.

And the guy's wife answers the door. "I've brought your husband home from the bar," Jim says to her.

"Thanks," she says. "That's great. But," looking around, "where's his wheelchair?"

When it was late enough I used the men's room in the bar to wash up and get ready to sleep and then I went to the Market Square Arena parking lot. When I'm in town and it's not too cold, a good place to sleep is on the highest covered floor of a parking lot. Tops of parking lots are good because late at night nobody else goes up there except couples who have no place else they can go and, for sure, they don't have it in mind to get out and study who might be settling down to sleep in the shadows. So we leave each other alone.

And sometimes, especially when it's in the summer and maybe they have a convertible, you can get quite an eyeful if the moon's out.

I always hope it's going to be someone famous, a politician or someone on Eyewitness News, but it never is. At least I've never recognized one from what I could see. Not that I am in any way thinking about blackmail. That wouldn't even occur to me. To tell the truth, one of the reasons I went into business was to keep on the legal side of life because I had a bad time in solitary in Detroit, which they put me into even though it wasn't my fault. Solitary was no more than a cage and I realized I never wanted to go back to jail again. To be sure of that I knew I had to get out of Detroit, even though I didn't have any money to do it with.

It gives me a buzz to see famous people. I see them walking around town sometimes. When that happens I go to the same part of the sidewalk I saw them on. The last famous person I saw was Danny Quayle, when he was the Indiana Vice President. I saw him on the Circle when there was a city children's party and he was coming out of a White Castle tent. I went and stood exactly where I saw him stand.

I like to think about sharing a space with a famous person, maybe even breathing in some of the air they just breathed out, like success was catching. They're no different from me really. I believe you can make yourself a success if you work at it, and that's one of my business philosophies. But it's also true that a break or two, here or there, does no harm, like being born the right place.

I was born in a bathtub, as a matter of fact.

My momma, Hettie, was a fat woman. I mean really big and she was having a bath and then she felt me coming. But she couldn't get up and there was only my sister Cissy that could hear her, and Cissy wasn't but two years old. So Momma, she just lay there and out I came, under the water, though the suds had died down.

They say I didn't cry, even when Momma got me up, and she thought I was dead. But then I opened my eyes and opened my mouth and took a breath of fresh air and I've been breathing fresh air ever since.

Still, it's no surprise I've never seen a famous person in a parking lot. Famous people are going to have special places to do it and not need parking lots, just like they've got special places to sleep.

* * *

I woke up with this great idea.

Now I think maybe if I'd slept further away, say in the parking lot next to the Hilton Hotel, maybe the longer walk would have been a chance for me to think it out better, including the risks. But as it was, the Market Square Arena is right across the street from the Police Department, so all I had to do was cross Alabama and go in the main door and ask to see somebody. And that's what I had the idea to do.

Inside the front door at the Police Department is a lobby with chairs and telephones, but there's a booth that blocks the way to the elevators and the rest of the building. The booth has two guys and they look about ten feet tall because the inside of the booth is raised up. That's one of the little tricks the police have, to make you scared if you aren't used to it, but not me.

"I want to see somebody," I said.

"Who is it that you want, sir?"

"A detective. It's got to be a detective."

I had a real bad time from an ordinary cop when I was young and I never, ever, have to do with them anymore if I can help it. In fact for years I tried not to talk to cops at all, but you can't go through a whole life like that. In the end, they are a part of life and they can even be a part of business, if you handle them right.

"Sir?"

"Yeah?"

"What's it about?"

"It's about a crime," I said. "I've got something important to say."

Then the second cop poked the one I was talking to and whispered something. They both looked at me, and the way they did it reminded me of times I've used the john in the bus station at night where the only door that locks is on the disabled toilet and it's sometimes occupied so you have to try another one only it's occupied too. It was not friendly.

The second guy squinted down like he couldn't see me under his shaggy eyebrows and he said, "What's your name?"

"Jan. Jan Moro."

"You sure you ain't called Starch?"

"Who?" I said.

"You sure do remind me of a little guy with a mustache named Clarence Starch that made a nuisance last spring. You even got the same color jacket."

"Never heard of him," I said. "And I never had a mustache."

Truth was I did used to have a mustache which I shaved to make me cleaner-looking which can help business. But the guy in the booth was a patrolman so I kept it simple for him.

He frowned at me, but he turned to the first guy and shrugged. He said, "Who do you think? Proffitt?"

The first guy said, "Proffitt sees anybody," so he picked up a phone. "What's it about again?"

"A crime," I said.

Proffitt was not a real big cop, thin with black hair and maybe thirty-five, and his suit looked comfortable, not rumpled, so it was a good one. He met me out of the elevator. "Mr. Moro?"

"Hi."

"I'm Detective Sergeant Proffitt. The boys downstairs tell me you have some information about a crime?"

He said his words like he'd come up from the country but in Indy you can't trust that to mean someone's stupid. "A crime, that's right," I said.

"You want to follow me down to an interview room?"

We walked down the hall and when we got settled he said, "If it's about a crime, I'd like to tape-record what you have to say, Mr. Moro."

"I'd rather you didn't. Look what happened to Nixon."

He didn't seem surprised. "All rightie." He took out a notebook. "What's up?"

"It's about puppies," I said.

"Puppies?"

"Young dogs."

6.

I told Proffitt about the dog business and how I was out for an early-morning walk when I saw the truck going into the back side of the Fairgrounds and that seemed funny to me so I followed it in.

As soon as I said about the Fairgrounds he looked like he was paying extra attention, but I put it down to the Fairgrounds being one of the famous places in town. Whatever it was, it was then he began to write stuff down.

I went through the story just about how it happened, especially about the suffering dogs, but I shortened it down. "And they called the boss Mr. Cobb. When I got dragged inside I told him I wanted a job but he had this guy called Pete who was one of his sidekicks lock me in the john."

Proffitt wrote down about that and I waited till he caught up.

"In the john there was a little window big enough for me to squeeze through, so I legged it. But I tell you, this Cobb is a monster-looking guy and that Pete may be pretty old, but he made a special point to tell me how he's eaten human flesh."

Proffitt made a face at that.

"I don't mind telling you, Mr. Proffitt, I was scared. Not many people scare me, but that guy Cobb, and that guy Pete, both of them, they did. You can tell dangerous guys, and both of them, they are dangerous guys."

Proffitt looked up from his notebook and leaned back.

"Is something wrong?" I asked.

"I'm thinking about what you've told me, Mr. Moro," he said. And he did. He thought. I watched him.

Finally he said, "You weren't just on an early-morning walk."

It surprised me that he sounded so sure. I said, "I wasn't?"

"You were either planning a burglary or on your way home from a burglary, isn't that right?"

"That is not right!" I said. "I am a law-abiding businessman, and nothing else, and that's the truth."

"I like the truth," Proffitt said. "So tell me why were you there."

You have to give in order to get sometimes. I said, "There's a guard's hut just inside the fence and now and then it's a handy place to sleep."

"So you slept there last night?"

"Until the truck came in."

"O.K., Mr. Moro, I understand what you've said, but what I don't understand is the crime you're reporting."

"I'm not a law expert," I said, "but it's got to be wrong to truck cute little puppies around that way, no room to move and all boxed up like that."

"So, you're reporting cruelty to animals?"

"For a start, yeah."

"Did anybody harm these dogs physically?"

"They were moaning like to bring tears to your eyes. If you'd heard them, you'd know they weren't happy."

"But you didn't see anyone, say, hit a dog or kick it?"

"Look, Mr. Proffitt," I said, "you go out there. You find out what they're up to and, sure as can be, you're going to find illegal stuff going on. Those guys are criminals. You can tell it just by looking at them."

"We need a little bit more than how somebody looks to get a conviction these days, Mr. Moro."

"You check it out, I'm sure you won't be disappointed."

"All right, I will see what I can come up with, I promise. Thanks for coming in." He got up. But I wasn't finished with him, even though he thought I was.

I said, "My idea was that I can help you check it out."

Proffitt looked down at me. "Just how did you have it in mind to help me, Mr. Moro?"

"If it would assist justice and make sure those poor little creatures get treated the way any animal deserves, I am willing to take the risk of going back there."

"For what purpose?"

"I could keep watch on those guys and report what I see. I could investigate into the setup they have so you'll have more information to start an investigation of your own."

He sat down again. "It doesn't sound safe for you to go out there after what happened yesterday, Mr. Moro."

"I won't get caught."

"You did the last time."

"When I know I got to be careful, I'm good at not being seen."

"Are you saying that you want to become a police informant?"

It was crunch time. I said, "Being a snitch is not my normal line of country, but, on the other hand, if it worked out and if I found things you could use, then maybe you could see your way to help me keep myself going on it. I'm not trying to make it expensive, but I'm sure I'd see and hear things that you'd want to know about."

"So, what you want is to become a paid police informant?"

There it was: my great idea. A way to make the dog business into business for me.

"You'll get good information," I said.

Proffitt closed his notebook and leaned back. Even so he kept looking straight at me. I'd made my pitch and he was deciding and he was letting me know he was deciding. I've seen how these country boys operate. My daddy was one and so were a lot of his friends.

After a while he said, "I can't authorize this on my own."

That was a lie, but I said, "You can't?"

"To prevent abuse of the paid informant relationship, we have a system here at IPD. Every informant has to be listed on a confidential file and given an identification number. And there is a procedure for determining the scale of financial remuneration."

"So what happens now?"

"I need you to be patient, Mr. Moro, while I tell my superiors everything you've told me."

He was giving me the runaround. I know guys who got signed up as informants quick as snapping a twig, so I said, "Are you going to do anything about those puppies or not? If you aren't, I think maybe I'll go to the *Star*, because it's criminal the pain and the agony those poor dogs are going through."

"Their suffering gets worse every time you speak of them, Mr. Moro," Proffitt said.

"It purely rendered my heart. I told you how they wailed."

He said, "Mr. Moro, I don't think it's a good idea for you to go to the newspapers."

"No?"

"If you do that, how could you function undercover for us?"

"It didn't sound like you wanted me to function for you." Then for good measure I said, "I only want to see justice done."

"I will talk to my superiors, I promise you."

"When?"

"As soon as I can, but meanwhile I think it's best that you stay away from the Fairgrounds, don't you?"

I had other things planned anyway but I said, "Why?"

"Number one, it's risky for you out there. Number two, if we do go ahead with this, my superiors will want to work the whole plan out before anything gets done."

"Well, I guess I can wait a little."

Proffitt said, "Now, how do I get in touch with you?"

"Being between jobs I don't have an address and I can't afford a room. And until you have an address—well, you know how it works."

Proffitt took out his wallet and gave me a ten dollar bill. Then he wrote something in his notebook. "Would you sign this receipt, please, Mr. Moro?"

"I'd rather not," I said. "Taxes. You know."

He sat looking at me, which made me feel uncomfortable, but he wrote something in the notebook himself and said, "You can get a bed for that at the Cape. You know the Cape?"

Everybody knows the Cape, but I said, "I'll have to see if they've got space."

"They always have space. Flophouses don't get a whole lot of convention business."

"If you want your money back . . ."

"I'm not checking up on you, but I want to know where I can find you after I've talked to my superiors."

"Well," I said, "I may be at the Linger Longer Lounge for a while later on tonight. You could try me there."

You'd have thought I shot the guy the way he jumped. "What the *hell* will you be doing in the Linger Longer Lounge?"

"Business," I said.

"What kind of 'business'?"

"I've got something to talk to the owner about, not that it's any concern of yours." You've got to draw the line with cops, so they don't think they own you.

He took the point I was making because he thought some

before he said, "It's not the sort of place I expected you to hang out, Mr. Moro, that's all."

"I don't hang out there."

"Look, maybe the best thing is if you give me a call in the morning. How about that? You can wait on this till the morning, can't you?"

"Yeah, all right," I said.

"If you do become an informant we'll give you an official identification number to protect your identity. Meanwhile when you call, ask for me and say you are 'one thousand and one.' "

"One thousand and one," I said. "Right."

He took a card out of his pocket and passed it over. "You make sure and give me that call, hear?"

"Is the number there smudged?" I said. "Or is it just too small for me to read without my glasses?"

He read the number out to me to make sure I had it right, and I put the card in my pocket.

7.

From the Police Department I went to the City Market, which is only across a street. City Market looks old and plain from the outside but it has lots of small food businesses in it, both fresh food and cooked to eat.

Later in the day it's a place there are good things thrown away behind, but this time I went for breakfast. Ten bucks is no fortune, but it was a start to the day, and my betting was more business might come from Detective Sergeant Proffitt. Quite often I'm right in my betting about people. I don't trust police promises, but it was a good sign he didn't want me to tell the newspapers about the dogs.

I bought a breakfast and carried it up to the tables on the mezzanine. Hunger's a good thing for eating. I took my time and enjoyed all the tastes on my tongue.

Then I saw a guy I knew and I called him over. He is

known as Beads because he wears beads in his hair. "Hey, man," he said, and he sat down.

I had an extra large coffee, which is the best value, so I shared it, which he appreciated, because not everyone would share a drink with him.

Beads is on the streets, but I have time for him because he knows I'm not the same as he is.

"Damn fine cup of coffee," he said.

"You on to anything today?"

He wrinkled up his nose and said, "Naw. It's quiet. How about you?"

I shook my head.

He said, "Hey, you hear about Creepy Kathy?"

"What about her?"

"She woke up dead."

"No!"

"Sure did. You know she likes it around them holes?"

He meant the construction holes that are the fashion downtown nowadays. "Yeah?"

"Well they found her in one of those."

"When was that?"

He thought to work it out. "No longer than the day before yesterday. Remember the cold night? It was that one, not that the cold got her."

"What then?"

"She wasn't well, not well at all, Kathy."

"That's too bad," I said.

"Coming our way to us all," Beads said. We shared a moment about that and then he stood up. "Got to move, man, got to move." And he left.

I was sorry about Creepy Kathy. It wasn't long ago that she was fine, but Beads was right, last time I saw her she was coughing and looking pale.

Kathy wasn't always on the streets—well, who is? The story I remember her telling me was about a mind-reading act she used to do with a one-legged guy.

How you do it is you get a crowd together, and you have them each write a question on a piece of paper and fold it up and put it in a hat. The mind reader picks one question paper out and he mind-reads what the question is through his fingertips just by touching it. Then he answers the question. It's a good act and can be amazing and Kathy said her and the one-legged guy made good money for a while at places like the State Fair or half-time of a football game where crowds are easy to find.

The trick of it is to have a shill to start you off. When the mind reader's holding up the first question out of the hat he might say, "This is from somebody named Nancy and she wants to know if she should say yes to marrying Elmer."

"That's me! I'm Nancy," the girl shill screams. "How did you know about Elmer? How embarrassing!"

"It's all in the power of my marvelous fingers," the mind reader says and he waves his fingers around.

Then he answers the question, and he opens the piece of paper to show the crowd it really had something written on it. Of course what that piece of paper has is a real question written by somebody else. Then the mind reader picks another paper out of the hat and all he has to do is remember the question off the first paper when he's feeling the new one with his marvelous fingers.

It's a good business if you've got a mind reader with a memory and he's got the style to carry it off. You make the money after the show, when people believe you've got the power and come up and pay for help with their other problems.

Kathy said the one-legged guy had a great style, but the act broke up when he put his marvelous fingers to a different kind of work and she couldn't stand for it anymore.

But that was just one thing that happened to Kathy, and then circumstances got to her and in the end she had no place but the streets and the holes to put her head down.

Because I was already there I went out back of the Market after breakfast, but it was too early to find anything good, so I carried on my plan and walked across town to the bus station and I left my sleeping bag and file in a locker since I was coming back later.

Then I used the johns and cleaned myself up. It felt good, that morning. I remember it. I felt fresh and it was good to be alive, already having done some business. And I was glad that Rosie was coming back, because she'd been away just about all the summer.

When Rosie is away she's with her little sister, Tulip, that lives in Chicago but is sick a lot. Part of the time Tulip travels for her health and she likes Rosie to come along for that too, to Florida, and to Arizona once, and up in Michigan in the summer.

Tulip was the lucky sister whose husband got rich and died. Tulip has children and grandchildren that could maybe look after her, but she counts on Rosie, who knows her little ways. And Tulip gives her money for it, though it's always "a present," and so when Rosie gets home she always has the cash to buy supplies for me to do some repairs to her house.

Rosie's husband only died. All he left behind was a little frame house on 24th Street and it always has repair and improvement things that need to be fixed and she can't do them for herself. Owning a house is no picnic, especially when you're away from it so much of the time.

I met up with Rosie in a laundromat. It's been about four years now. Rosie put this quarter in a candy machine but it wouldn't put out the candy and then she couldn't get the quarter back either. That made her mad and she kicked the machine, but that only hurt her toe.

I was waiting for a dryer, myself, but I heard her say, "Shit!" and I went over to help out. I carry some sticky tape in my file and I stuck a piece to the quarter and eased it out that way. So naturally we got to talking.

Rosie was just about the most dressed-up woman I ever saw doing her laundry, though to talk to she wasn't snooty and I'll talk to just about anyone. But I told her she was a surprising-looking woman to be in a laundromat, and she liked that because she said she was only there because her washing machine wouldn't pump out.

Well, I cheered her up and made her laugh by telling her a couple of stories, and I helped her learn about working the machines. After a while she said she was having a better time in the laundromat than anywhere else in town and that was when she told me about this son she has that lives in Indy but they don't speak.

In fact, I went back to her house with her that same day, which is a testament to my philosophy of keeping clean. Later on she said she was sure she was safe with a man she met in a laundromat if he turned away when she loaded her lingerie. What I went to her house for was to look at her washing machine. And then, when I fixed it which showed I was handy, we became good friends.

To tell the truth, Rosie also likes it that I am about less than half her age. We never go back to a place where a waiter calls me her son. But Rosie can be a warm, warm woman, even though she'd never get private without making up her face and it being in the dark.

I never stay in her house when she's not there because that would be like I had moved in, but nowadays we always fix it up so that I know when she's due back from Tulip's. I meet her and I carry her bags and we have a little party.

This time she was coming back the Thursday on the bus that gets in from Chicago at two-thirty, unless it was the Friday instead.

After I cleaned up, there was still a lot of day before two-thirty. I got the idea to go over to the *Star* and test out how they'd like cruelty to cute little puppies, just in case Proffitt didn't come through.

On the way over I got to thinking about Proffitt. At first he was setting up to get rid of me and not care about what I was telling him, I'm sure of that. But then he changed his mind. What puzzled me was that I wasn't sure if my saying I'd go to the newspapers was what really made the difference.

At the *Star* what I did at one of the counters was ask what to do if I had a good story for them. I got sent up to Reception at the editorial department. There I talked to a kid with a crew cut who said his name was Dave. "So let me get this straight," he said. "You're researching a feature?"

"You got it."

"And once you've completed your research you want what? To write it up for us?"

"What I thought would be best was that I would see one of your reporters and he or she would know what to do. What is my specialty is getting the facts up together, but I don't claim to be a good enough writer to write it for the newspaper myself."

"What story exactly is it you're researching?" he asked.

I laughed. "You're not going to get me that way, Dave."

"I wasn't trying to horn in, Mr. Moro, honest."

"Do I look that green? All I can say is it's about guys involved in crimes."

"Oh!"

"And they're also abusing animals."

"That's awful," Dave said, and his voice had real feeling behind it which I took to be a good sign. "What kind of animals? What are they doing to them?"

"It's puppies," I said.

Dave looked about to faint. Suddenly I heard Al's voice in my head saying, "Pin a curly tail on him." So I said to Dave, "There may be other animals too. Maybe pigs and donkeys."

"Oh how terrible! And you want to talk to one of our feature writers? Is that it?"

"Not right now, but I will once I have all the facts."

"You'll make sure to double-check them, I hope."

"Right. Or triple."

"So what is it you want today, Mr. Moro? Access to the morgue?"

I didn't understand what the morgue had to do with it, but Dave was really interested, so I said, "To tell the truth, I'm having a certain amount of trouble meeting my research expenses."

And suddenly Dave wasn't interested anymore.

Oh well. You can only try, which is another of my philosophies.

Rosie wasn't on the two-thirty bus.

I spent the afternoon nursing a couple of beers in a bar I know up Illinois, but nobody came in that seemed like he would make a good mind reader and all the stories were ugly ones, about hurting people, and I didn't get the point.

8.

It was well after dark before I began to think ahead again, about Billy Cigar and the Linger Longer Lounge. What I did was leave the bar and walk back to the bus station and that cleared my head.

I took my stuff out of the locker and then washed my good shirt, and my tie, in the restroom. They dried all right under one of the hot air machines between the sinks but to get a press on them I needed a seat in the waiting part of the main concourse. I tried the TV chairs first but none had time left so instead I sat on my clothes where I could see the photo booth and the giant gumball machine. Some folks might think sitting in a bus station is boring, but for me there's hardly a better show in town than a bus station with all the people and the pieces of conversations and the hustles for money.

Some places you can watch how the beggers keep an eye on

one another. If one guy scores some change, the mark won't hardly get ten steps before the next guy is up there with a more miserable story than the last. Once in Detroit I saw a college-looking kid dip into his pocket five times before he got to the street. All the sob stories he was hearing, I was surprised he didn't leave the place in tears. Of course some guys just stick a hand out without a story, but I could never do that.

This time I saw a pickpocket who was working alone. He was dressed well enough and went down the ticket line bumping into people with the idea being for them to take him for a drunk. But from where I was sitting I saw him lift a wallet from a woman's open purse.

At another time in my life I might have taken him aside and scared him into a cut, because if he was that obvious, he deserved whatever happened and it would do him a good lesson in the long run. But that's not my philosophy anymore, and anyhow I didn't want to come back and find my shirt and tie gone off the chair.

I also saw a little country gal come in from the buses with two big brown eyes and a cheap suitcase. She wandered in and stopped in the middle of the room and looked around and quicker than you could clap a hand there was a guy come up to her with a smile and in a minute he was carrying her bag towards the doors. I've helped gals that way in my time too, which is not something I am proud of now, but one thing getting older does is mature you.

The little gal accepted help from the friendly stranger. Well, maybe that's what she was looking for or maybe it wasn't, but for me this was a business night so there was no getting involved. I had my plans at the Linger Longer Lounge and on the way I'd drop my things by the ventilation ducts on the fifth floor of the Market Square Arena parking lot. They empty the trash barrels every twelve hours there but things are safe by the vents.

By wearing a tie this time, I'd get past Ed at the front door and the worst that could happen while I checked the place out was that a drink would cost me the rest of Proffitt's money.

Funny, sitting there, the taste of a tequila sunrise came into my head. Now, that's not a taste I would come home from a foreign country for, but I got hit by a strong hankering there in the bus station.

I had my first tequila sunrise in Lansing, not Mexico. I was in a bar and it was summer and I saw a white butterfly trying to get out a window, so I opened the window up and out the butterfly flew. And it wasn't hardly a moment's flash before a big old bird flew by and caught the little thing and that was that. It made me feel about *so* big.

Well, there was a woman name of Kaye behind the bar and she saw what happened and she whipped up this drink and said, "There you go, son, try that," and that was my first tequila sunrise. Kaye had big wet beautiful brown eyes like the little country gal, so maybe that's what put me in mind of a tequila sunrise.

I changed shirts and tied my tie in the restroom. When I combed my hair I caught myself in the mirror and I liked how good I was looking, not tired from the day. Some days nighttime is my time.

I left the restroom thinking that "nighttime is my time" sounded pretty poetic. I didn't know if I had made it up or if I was just remembering it from somewhere else, but I got the idea that it would be good to fit into a song sometime. And that got me to thinking about my plan that I have for a public access TV show.

I should have been getting ready to talk to Billy Cigar, but I wasn't. I should have been thinking up how to explain the deodorant for clothes and the smoking hood too, but you can't always help what you're thinking and I hummed myself all the way to the parking lot and it was after nine when I started out for the Linger Longer. Only I never got there.

I was walking along the street humming and doing a few

dance steps now and then and I didn't give as much attention as I do sometimes to who was in the parked cars along the way. What I remember is hearing a car door open across the street, but so what? Doors got to open, birds got to fly.

Then, there was someone running. I turned around and I saw a couple of guys coming my way. Well, nobody but a jogger runs that doesn't have to, so I stepped out of their path and into the street, but the guys changed direction, and by the time I realized they were running after me, they had me.

The first one I managed to kick in the vicinity of his chachas but the second guy grabbed me tight on the arm. I fought him as hard as I could and said, "Get off! Get off!"

He said, "Mr. Moro, it's O.K."

I looked up and it was Detective Sergeant Proffitt. I tried to shake his hand off again, but he wouldn't turn loose. I said, "What you want to scare a guy like that for? Jeez Louise!"

"We need to talk to you, Mr. Moro."

The guy who was holding his crotch said, "I'll fucking talk to him."

I said, "So talk."

"Not here," Proffitt said.

"Look, if you want me to forget the puppies, I'll forget them, all right? No hard feelings. But I've already spent the ten bucks."

"It's more complicated than that," Proffitt said and they walked me to their car and made me get in the back sitting in the middle. There was a third guy in the driver's seat already and he started the car up.

"This is kidnapping," I said.

"We're not going far," Proffitt said.

"I don't want to go anywhere at all."

"Shut up!" Chachas said. He was still holding himself, so it must have been a pretty good shot for off the cuff.

I said, "There's a ridge down the middle of this seat and it's not comfortable."

"I'm real sorry about that," Proffitt said.

"How long is this going to take? Because I've got a business appointment. If I lose out on a lot of money, you guys are going to have to make it up to me."

Proffitt turned his head my way. "Mr. Moro, we've got it in mind to give you some money anyway, so y'all just hush up for a couple of minutes, hear?"

That hushed me up all right. I sat back and thought of money and tried to work out what could be going on.

Where we went was only about five blocks from the Linger Longer. It was in an alley under a light behind a church and there was a car waiting for us. We pulled up behind it and Proffitt said, "You guys get some air, O.K.?"

The driver said, "Cloak and dagger, huh?" but he and Chachas both got out.

The guy from the other car got into ours, next to me in the back seat. He was heavy and black and about fifty with short curly hair going gray. The way he looked at me shouted "Cop!" till I was deaf.

He said, "Any problems, Homer?"

"No, sir," Proffitt said.

The new guy said, "Mr. Moro, I'm Captain Miller."

"What's all this about, Captain? Because these guys kidnapped me off a public street while I was on the way to a business appointment. Are you charging me with something? Because if you are, I didn't do it."

"It's nothing like that, Mr. Moro," Miller said.

"What is it like?" I said.

"This afternoon Sergeant Proffitt told me about the incident of abuse to puppy dogs you reported to him."

"That's right," I said. "I did."

"What Sergeant Proffitt told me touched my heart, Mr. Moro, it really did. And what particularly impressed me was the genuine concern you expressed about the puppies' welfare."

It was hard to see where this was leading, but if you don't want to fall, you got to run with the ball. I said, "I think anybody who heard or saw those poor creatures would have been as upset as me."

"But not everyone would have made the effort to report it," Miller said. "I truly commend you."

"I try to be a good citizen," I said. "And if you're going to give me a medal, could you hurry up, because, see, I have someplace I've got to go."

"It must be puzzling you as to why we arranged this meeting," Miller said.

Kidnap is not what I call arranging, but I didn't say that. "Well, on the way over here Sergeant Proffitt did mention about giving me some money."

"We have a proposition to put to you, Mr. Moro," Miller said. "We all want to help those poor little puppies, but at the same time we know you probably have expenses to meet."

"I sure do."

Proffitt said, "We've been thinking about your offer to watch the goings-on out at the Fairgrounds."

"You want me to keep an eye on those guys with the dogs? Is that it?"

"That's right, Mr. Moro," Miller said. "But only for as long as you are able to do it without any chance of being seen by any of the people working there. Because there's no way that I want you to put yourself at risk. They already threatened you, I believe."

"They did," I said.

Miller said, "So you must promise that you will do absolutely nothing that might lead to your being discovered. There's the personal risk to yourself, and also the fact that if they get wind that they're being watched, we'll lose our chance to bust the whole operation."

"Do you know what their business with the dogs is?"

"No," Proffitt said. "Could be just about anything, though. Even raising dogs for meat."

That was one I hadn't thought of, and it would explain why the puppies were so big. "So what do you want me to do?" I said.

Proffitt said, "Set yourself up in that hut you told me about, and keep track of all the cars and trucks you see, how big they are, license plates, people in them, everything."

"And?"

"We'll give you thirty dollars a night, with a bonus of a hundred when the job's over, but only if nobody there sees you."

"How long would you want me to do this for?"

"We can't be sure, but even if it's just tonight, we'll guarantee the hundred."

"I don't know," I said.

"Is there a problem?" Miller said. "I thought this is what you offered to do."

"How did you plan to pay me?"

"Sergeant Proffitt will meet you every morning, somewhere near the Fairgrounds. You'll tell him what you've seen the night before and he'll give you the thirty dollars."

"Why is it nights you want me out there?"

"If what they're doing is illegal, that's when they're most likely to ship the animals in and out. Nights and the early mornings, like today."

I could have asked how they knew that if they didn't know what the business was, but I just said, "Oh," and nodded.

"If Sergeant Proffitt sees you first thing, it'll give you the whole day to get supplies and do your own business, as long as you're back on watch by five. So, how does that sound?"

"I'll need more than thirty dollars," I said.

They looked at each other. "How much?" Miller said.

"At least fifty a night, and twenty-five up front."

Miller took a breath but he said, "All right, fifty. As long as you start tonight."

"You've got a deal," I said.

Miller and Proffitt drove me out to the Fairgrounds. I didn't want to show them the hole that I cut to get through the fence, so I had to climb the gate. That was awkward, and I was afraid I would mess my shirt up, but I took it slow and got over in one piece. The two of them stood by the fence till they saw me go inside the guard's hut.

The whole deal stank like pigsty, of course, but I had another twenty-five bucks in my pocket and I didn't much care what they were really up to.

When I was sure they were gone I set out back to town. One reason was to pick up my sleeping bag and file, but another was my business at the Linger Longer Lounge. A job for the cops was one thing, and getting cash money up front was most ways to a miracle, but if I could get Billy Cigar interested in my slow-release deodorant, that had the potential to make me rich for life.

9.

I did not go to the street entrance of the Linger Longer, though it was a temptation. I liked the idea of tipping Ed a dollar and saying, "Thank you, my man," when he opened the door. I've seen that in movies and it would tickle me to do it and I don't do my business at clubs with an awning and a doorman very often and that's where the temptation came in. But at the same time I had a suspicion that Proffitt and Miller might be waiting someplace along the street, to check up on me. They'd done it the once, so I came up to the club along the alley at the back.

I hung around for a while in the parking lot there and it wasn't long before a guy from the kitchen dumped some bags in one of the garbage cans. The door he came through was on a spring and shut behind him, but the guy didn't need a key to get back inside. After a couple of minutes I went to the door. I didn't hear anything, so I walked in. If I'd been stopped, I'd have said I parked my car out back and thought this was the way in.

What I found behind the door was an empty corridor with green linoleum on the floor. I could hear the kitchen off to the right, and I heard music straight ahead. I walked towards the music. I passed a short corridor on the left that led to what might be a couple of offices and where Billy might be, but I kept on going to a door that I guessed led to the main part of the club.

This door had a complicated steel-and-plastic lock on it, but there was also a handle so I tried that. The door opened right up and I saw that the steel and plastic was the back side of one of those combination door locks, but the combination was on the other side, not mine. And there I was, inside the Linger Longer Lounge.

Just off to the right was the men's room. I went in. I washed my hands and straightened my tie and walked casually back into the lounge, like it was where I belonged.

There was a reasonable crowd, but not packed. In front of me were tables that had some people eating, but the biggest numbers were at a long bar that curved like a horseshoe around one whole end of the room. Between the legs of the horseshoe were some smaller tables that were maybe for people drinking without food.

Up the other end of the lounge, in a corner, there was a stage with a live band. Ed said there was a big act with a cover charge coming in on Saturday, so I hadn't expected live music tonight, but there were three of them and it was live all right. The sound of the band was prairie rock, which I liked because one of the songs I'm working on is a prairie rock song. It's about being lonesome, but the tune isn't slow.

I work on my songs singing in my head as I'm settling down to sleep, if I'm not thinking about something else. My lonesome song isn't finished, but if this band being in the club showed that prairie rock was what Billy Cigar liked, then having part of a prairie rock song was maybe a way to start up a conversation.

Making the first contact is very important in business. If how I contacted him was wrong, a guy like Billy Cigar might even have me thrown out of the club if that was his mood. And that way we could both lose a lot of money. But if it was right, he'd look at me and listen, and be interested.

I didn't know yet how I was going to make my approach, because you can't plan everything about a circumstance. But I'd thought about a lot of things as maybes.

What I did was go to one end of the bar to get a beer. But no sooner did I get myself a place than I spotted Billy Cigar himself, right across from me, standing at the other end of the bar. That got me scared and excited, all at the same time. I truly hadn't expected to find Billy in the club, not at my very first time of being there.

He was talking with four guys that all had cowboy hats on. They were laughing and slapping backs and I knew right away it was a circumstance that if I went up and said, "Excuse me, Mr. Cigar, I want to talk a little business with you," he would look down and say, "Who is this jerk?"

But Billy being there in the club was too lucky a chance to throw away. What I had to do was keep an eye open for my opportunity, even though I knew that it might not come that night. Business is business and the bigger the deal, the worse it is if you try to force it.

My beer came and I sat on a stool where I could watch Billy, and I tried to be patient and calm down. I needn't have hurried to relax, though, because it was more than half an hour before the cowboy hats patted Billy on the back for the last time and left him alone.

And there he was, by himself, not thirty feet away. By himself and not looking like he was about to go somewhere. It was hard to believe. But you've got to take your chances, they may not come back, so I eased off my stool and headed straight for him.

But before I got there, a tall guy with a tan, and two women with him, they all got up from a drinks table and they went over to Billy and they got to him first. The guy was in an expensive suit and he also had a lot of gold jewelry—tie pin and bracelet and a watch and rings. He shook hands with Billy and he seemed to know him and then he introduced one of the women, who was blond-haired with lots of little-girl curls and a red dress.

I could have turned around, but I'd been having some luck already so I decided to order another beer over their side of the bar and see if I could listen in on what they were saying.

When I walked past, I heard the gold jewelry guy say, ". . . couldn't believe someone as handsome as you used to be a cop," and the blond-haired woman in the red dress say, "Ramón, you're a pig to tell him that!"

Well, that told me something about the blond-haired woman because handsome was not the first word I would have used to describe Billy, though it's true that my taste is not everybody's.

I found myself a place at the bar only a couple of yards away and I eased myself even closer before I caught a bartender's eye. When I'd ordered my beer I turned my mind back to Billy and I heard him say, "So I came home early and what did I find? Another fucking cop! In *my* house, with *my* wife!"

"No!" the blond woman said. From what I was told two days before I worked out that this must be a story about Billy's wife before Linda, the one he had when he was a cop himself in San Diego.

"Well, one thing led to another," Billy said, "and the other fella lit out and I lit out after him and, by God, I sure as hell caught up with him."

"What did you do?" the blond woman asked, and I could tell she was the loose one of the two, meaning that it was the other woman who was with Ramón. The loose woman had her eye on Billy, that was for sure.

Billy said, "I pulled my gun and he pulled his gun and let's just say that there was a meaningful exchange."

"Gosh!" the loose woman said.

"Oh, weren't nobody hurt," Billy said. "But I made damn sure he wouldn't be driving to anybody else's house in *that* car again."

The loose woman laughed.

Billy said, " 'Course the bastard didn't like that, and he put it out on the radio that he was under fire, not even keeping the business to ourselves. And that meant that within a couple of minutes we had just about every patrol car in town for company, and the next thing I knew *I* was being investigated."

"You?" the loose woman asked. "But what about the other guy?"

Billy looked from the loose woman to Ramón to the second woman, who I hadn't heard say a word, and back to the loose woman. He said, "I could see the fucking writing on the wall, so I quit the force before they fired me. And all that happened to the other cop was he got suspended for five days. Work that one out."

"But that's not fair!" the loose woman said.

"Ain't life a bitch? Hey honey, you got no drink," Billy said, and I could see that he was interested in her too.

And then I got this *great* idea. I picked up my beer and my change and I stepped between Billy and the loose woman, right in the middle.

I said, "Excuse me, Mr. Cigar. Sorry to butt in, but only two nights ago I was in a place and you bought everybody drinks. And I got to wondering if anybody ever buys you a drink. So I'd like to do that, buy you a drink, just to say thank you and then be on my way."

It stopped him cold.

"What will you have?" I said.

"Do I know you?"

"It was at Sam's Saloon," I said. "You were with two of your own guys. But I'm not trying to bust up your party. I'd just like to buy you a drink to show you my appreciation."

He made his decision. He said, "Well thanks, little fella." He put a hand on my shoulder and turned to the bartender. All it took was a nod.

I could hardly keep from whooping. I'd made my contact! Even if I didn't get to talk business tonight, as long as I got back to Billy soon enough—a day or two—he'd remember me as the little guy who bought him a drink and I'd be able to make my pitch.

But, no sooner had all that happened than fate stepped up and played a wild card. Another guy entirely came up to Billy. In fact, it was one of the guys he was with at Sam's. Billy saw him coming and he touched the blond woman on her elbow and he said, "Excuse me a sec, pretty lady. I'll be right back." Then he moved to one side and met the guy and they talked in low voices.

Meanwhile Billy's drink came, which turned out to be rye whiskey, and I paid for it.

I heard Billy say, "*Fucking* animals!" and I turned back and I saw he was making a fist.

The guy with Billy smiled, but he stepped back just the same. "That's what she said, boss. I'm just the errand boy."

Billy said, "All right, all right. Tell her I'm on my way," and then he came back to the rest of us. I handed Billy his drink and he said, "Thanks, son," to me.

"My pleasure," I said.

But before I could leave, Billy said to all four of us, "I've got to leave you now and go back to the office. My wife is bugging me to meet some goddamn clown and talk about animals."

The loose woman said, "Oh!" in a disappointed way.

Then Billy seemed to get an idea. He said, "Hey, we were getting along so well why don't you folks come back with me. We'll give Linda and her animal pal a nice little surprise party. Maybe pass the hat around and save a goddamn panda. How about that?"

Ramón said, "I think perhaps we don't interfere between a man and his wife, Billy." He was smiling as he said it. "However it was a pleasure to meet you again, wasn't it, girls?"

The loose woman stepped forward and stuck out her hand and she said, "I do hope I'll have a chance to get to know you better one day, Mr. Sigra."

Billy took her hand in both of his and he rubbed it with one of his thumbs. "Let's make it real soon, Barb. I really mean that."

"Me too," Barb said.

Billy let go her hand and said to Ramón, "Thanks for coming by and introducing me to this lovely lady. You sure you all won't come back and meet Linda?"

"Another time," Ramón said.

But I said, "Thanks, Mr. Cigar. That'd be nice."

Billy looked down at me for just a second, but then he said, "You got it, son. Let's go see what kind of weirdo she's drug up this time." And so in the end it was just Billy and me who crossed the lounge to the door with the combination lock.

I was about in heaven. I could hardly believe it. I figured my chances of getting to talk deodorant were going up with every single step.

10.

I followed Billy down the little corridor where I'd already thought the office might be. He went in the door at the end, and it turned out to be more of a living room than how I think of an office. There was a desk, but there were also easy chairs and a coffee table and a couch and a TV and a jukebox and a bar.

Linda was standing near the door and frowning. Even mad she was strikingly red-headed and a graceful-looking woman.

"Where the hell have you been?" she said.

Billy made a play of sniffing the air. He said, "Where's the fucking fire to haul me and my pal away from an important conversation?"

My pal!

"Hi," I said. I moved around from behind Billy and stuck out my hand. "Jan Moro. Pleased to meet you." Linda ignored me, but I didn't get a chance to think that through, because no sooner had I stepped into the room than I saw who else was inside. I could hardly believe it. In fact I didn't believe it at first. I doubted my own eyes, and that's not what I usually do because I have good eyes.

Getting up to be introduced to Billy Cigar was seven-toed Pete from the dog place.

Billy said, "I'm here now, all right? So what's the problem? Who's the guy?"

It was then that Pete saw me. He took just a blink to hesitate, but he moved to Billy and they shook hands. "Pete Yount," he said.

"Billy Sigra," Billy said. "And this is . . ."

I stepped forward and stuck my hand out. "Jan Moro, Mr. Yount. Glad to make your acquaintanceship."

And Pete and I shook hands.

Billy said to Linda, "At least give me a goddamn drink," and he dropped into one of the easy chairs.

Linda didn't look happy, but she went to the bar and poured him one from a whiskey bottle. Pete already had a drink where he was sitting and he sat back down. Linda didn't offer me one from being annoyed with Billy, but I sat down on the couch near Billy's chair.

When Billy had taken a big swig Linda said, "Mr. Yount has told me the most disgusting story."

Billy looked at Pete. "Do you get off on telling women disgusting stories, Yount?"

"Stop it, Billy!" Linda said sharply. "It's no joke. I can hardly bear to think about it."

"So what the fuck's it all about, Yount?"

It was hard to believe that this was the same guy who had looked so mean out at the Fairgrounds and who ate his own toes. He sat there in a suit and even his beard looked cleaner. He talked smoothly, and what he talked about was the dogs!

"I work for a man named Cobb," Pete said. "He's got a warehouse at the Fairgrounds and he told me it was for distributing puppies to pet shops. He does some of that, but in the last month what Cobb has started to do is train big dogs for fighting."

Linda said, "He trains them to kill pigs!"

Billy looked at her like she was crazy. "Kill pigs? You mean cops?"

"No! Don't be so stupid," Linda said.

Billy said, "What's killing pigs mean in English, Yount?" which was getting at Linda because she talked with an accent and had called him stupid.

Pete said, "Some of the dogs go to fight other dogs, but what Cobb trains for specially is to fight what's called 'dog and hog.' "

Linda said, "These poor dogs are put in a pen where they must fight against a huge pig to stay alive, and the pig has been especially bred from the jungle pigs with the big tusks."

"Wow!" Billy said. "I never heard of that."

"I have seen it," Linda said, "but I never thought to see it in *this* country."

"It came up from South America way," Pete said. "There's fighting circuits established in Texas but Cobb has the idea it'll catch on big up here because of all the pig farmers. He's already got breeders supplying him dogs called the *Doga argentina* and the *Fila braziliera*."

"Those are huge, huge vicious fighting dogs," Linda said.

"And he's got a hog breeder in Kentucky."

Linda said, "The fights make much gambling and much blood."

"Sounds like fun," Billy said.

"Billy!"

"Yeah, sorry. Just a joke."

"Is *not* funny," Linda said. She was really mad. Anybody could see that.

Billy put his feet up on the coffee table and took a drink. "So why are you here, Yount?"

"I can't take how Cobb trains the dogs," Pete said.

Linda said, "The dog is made hungry and then he puts it in a cage with a little piglet."

"There are machines he uses, too," Pete said. "He's got a whole system worked out."

"It's inhuman," Linda said.

"What gets me more than anything," Pete said, "is that the guy really enjoys the blood and watching the dogs go wild and rip the piglets to pieces."

Having met Cobb I could believe it. The guy was bad. You only had to look at him to know that.

"Billy," Linda said, "he even cooked a puppy in a microwave."

"Yeah?" Billy said.

Pete said, "The puppies come in and if they get sick or won't do what he wants, he kills them. This one he put into a microwave oven and cooked it to death and laughed and made everybody watch while it barked and clawed to get out. He said it was an experiment for a new kind of hot dogs. It's about the worst thing I've ever had to sit through."

We all sat there quiet for a moment, till Billy said to Linda, "Do we know anything about this Cobb?"

She shook her head.

He thought for a minute. Then he looked at Pete. "So you work for him, Yount?"

Pete said, "Yeah."

"But you don't like it."

"I hate it."

"So why not quit, or go to the cops?"

Pete smiled. "Me and the cops aren't exactly on speaking terms. But what happened was I read about this anticruelty thing in the paper. I called them up and they told me that Mrs. Sigra is one of their major supporters."

"So are a lot of other people," Billy said.

Pete didn't say anything at first and just scratched at his beard. Then he said, "I came here, Mr. Sigra, because most of those do-goody people, they think the way you solve a problem is to write a letter, if you know what I mean."

"Do I know what you mean?" Billy said.

"Come on, Mr. Sigra. Everybody knows about you. Everybody knows you're a guy who can sort out whatever he needs to. I'm not saying that dogs are top of your list, but I came here because I knew you could take care of the problem if you ever decided to."

"And where does that leave you and your job, Yount?"

"I'll make out. I always have."

Linda said, "Billy, that poor little dog in the microwave!" Billy put up his hand. She stopped talking.

"I still don't get it, Yount," Billy said.

"What don't you get?"

"If you don't care about losing your job, there are a hundred ways you could fuck up Cobb's business. Why come to Linda? Why come to me?"

"O.K.," Pete said. "I'll put it on the table."

"Not with a fucking lady present, you won't," Billy said, and he laughed enough for us all, even though we all laughed too.

Finally Pete said, "I think to myself, come to Billy Cigar and his missus and maybe I get sent away. But another thing that could happen is that they see I'm a guy who deals straight and maybe they decide they've got a job for me." Pete sat back. "There," he said. "That's the whole thing."

Billy nodded for just a moment. "O.K.," he said. "You're after a job. That makes more sense. So, how about you shove off now, Yount. Let us think about it."

Pete nodded. "Yes sir. Sure thing." He got up and went to the door.

Billy noticed me again. "I think maybe you better go too."

"Jan Moro," I said. "Yeah. We can talk about the clothes business another time. Maybe in a day or two."

"Yeah," Billy said. "Great."

And suddenly, there I was, in the corridor with Pete.

I guessed what was going to happen, but I couldn't move fast enough to do anything about it. No sooner was the door closed behind us than Pete grabbed me by the arm. And the guy was strong as hell. But before he could say one single thing, Billy Cigar's door opened up again and Billy stood there looking at us.

Pete said, "There you go, little fella. Hey, watch your step next time." And he let me loose.

Corny, but Billy bought it. He said, "I forgot to ask how we can contact you, Yount."

I didn't wait around to hear the answer.

11.

I went out the back. I picked up my sleeping bag and file from by the ventilation ducts at the parking lot, then I set out for the guard's hut at the Fairgrounds.

The walking gave me time to think. The whole of Pete was a real puzzle. I went through in my head how he had acted with Linda and Billy, and what he had said. For sure he was a more complicated person than the one who took his shoe and sock off in the john, but I was nowhere close to understanding it all.

Out at the dog place he'd been as mean as could be, but maybe it was all an act because he was scared of Cobb. Maybe he thought that Cobb was going to kill me, even though I was too big to fit in a microwave. That could explain why Pete wanted me to get away. Maybe I'd had a closer call than I thought. Maybe Cobb would have fed me to the dogs. Cobb was dangerous. No doubt about that.

And yet here I was spying on Cobb and his dog business, and I was doing it for the cops. People wake up dead doing the sort of thing I was doing and it was a reason to try Proffitt and Miller for bigger money.

Even though I didn't understand Pete himself, what he said about dogs fighting the special pigs explained why the puppies were so big. They hadn't seemed mean when I saw them in the back of the truck, but anything can be made vicious by circumstances. My own daddy is an example of that.

The only pigs I'd ever seen were sure more built for eating than for fighting, but I didn't doubt you could get pigs to be mean too. The pigs I saw were at my momma's folks' place, which was between Lima and Delphos in Ohio. It was also the only time I ever met Momma's people. They had two sows and a boar and some piglets.

I used to watch all the pigs through the fence, even though they smelled bad. They watched me too, and they had alligator eyes like they'd eat me along with everything else, if they ever got the chance. Funny thing was I wasn't afraid or anything, though I was only about nine. I really kind of liked them, which I couldn't say about the people inside the house. We only spent the two nights and all us kids had to sleep on the floor. Momma's mother cried all the time even though Momma's daddy told her again and again to stop it.

My own daddy wasn't there, because we came up and went back on the bus and we had to change a couple of times. That was me and Momma and Cissy and Wayne. This was when for the short time we all lived in a little rental house in Indy, where later that winter Momma got sick and died 'cause there was nobody there to take care of her.

Daddy's work was driving all over for some friend Momma didn't like and it got freezing cold. That day when us kids came back from school Momma was lying on her bed with up-chuck on her face and all over the pillow. We already knew she wasn't feeling good when we left her in the morning but she said, "Get along off with you," and wouldn't see no doctor and only took her own medicine which later Cissy said was making her a drunk.

Daddy didn't get home till two whole nights after we found her like that, but we didn't go to school the next day and just stayed with her instead so she wouldn't be alone. I kept brushing her hair like she used to let me do, and saying the funny words that made her laugh, but they didn't make her laugh that time.

And I recall Daddy finally walking in through the door and Cissy saying, "Momma's dead in bed," and him saying, "That's not funny," only it was me he hit instead of her.

And then all he could do was cry.

No, Daddy wasn't there, but I do remember the pigs and how they looked at me.

When I got out to the Fairgrounds, suddenly sleeping in the guard's hut didn't feel right to me. In fact it felt like I'd be doing a wrong thing.

The reason was Proffitt and Miller had told me to stay in the hut and spy from there. What was wrong was that I don't like anybody knowing just exactly where I am. Especially not cops.

So what I did was to set myself up in a mess of evergreen bushes along the wire fence, between the gate and where I cut the hole. The bushes were overgrown and straggly, and once I spread out, I was as comfortable as I would have been anywhere. It was like a nest and would have been O.K. even if it was raining or cold, neither of which it was.

From the bushes I could still see the gate, so I'd be able to keep track of everything coming in and out like the cops wanted. And I was even better protected from anybody seeing me.

I tried to settle down and get some sleep. But I couldn't do it. I was restless, from all the things that had happened. And the more I tried to sleep the more I got bad memories I hadn't thought about for years, like one time in a bar when I asked a guy what ever happened to another guy we both knew whose name was Young'un and he told me Young'un was dead.

Young'un was on the side of this office building, four floors up, with a friend of his doing a break-in. It was the middle of the night. Then the friend began to slip. Young'un reached out to steady him, but the friend grabbed Young'un's arm and the both of them fell off and died. The guy I talked to in the bar was the lookout on the sidewalk and he saw it all.

I hate it when I think about Young'un. Not because he was a great pal, though we spent three weeks living together once before he got released, but because it's about the worst thing in the world to try to help a guy and have him pull you to your death.

Then I started thinking about the dog in the microwave, so I stopped trying to sleep. What I did was get up and go for a walk down towards the dog warehouse.

I worked the shadows and took my time. Not that I thought anyone would be inside looking out at the scenery after midnight, but I had it in my mind to be careful. Proffitt and Miller said they wouldn't give me the hundred bucks bonus if I was ever spotted.

Not that I expected them to keep their word. Not cops. A cop was the biggest letdown in my whole life and that was when I was only thirteen years old.

There were no trucks or cars outside the warehouse. And no lights on. Since I was restless anyhow, I got the idea to go inside and have a look-see. The john window opened easy enough when I got out. I could shinny up and get back in just as easy. But to be on the safe side I walked all the way around the warehouse, really slow.

Even at night cities are light. There was a show on the TV in a bar I was in once that had this astronomer from Arizona complaining that the streetlights in Tucson screwed up his star-watching fifty miles away. It was interesting that streetlights could do that. Then someone changed the channel.

When I got to the john window, I went in. Inside, that was really dark. I took my time. I worked my way along the corridor by touch, and when I got to the main room Cobb and the others had been, I could use my smell too, because it smelled of instant coffee and fat from burgers. There were also dog smells in the air and that dry dogfood you add water to.

The only sound was from some dogs lowing in the warehouse room next door.

I didn't hurry myself at all. I worked my way around the room, touching pretty much everything, including the microwave, and after a while I found the door to the warehouse room. I could tell because the dog smell was strongest there.

I went in. As soon as I did, a howl started from one dog close to me and then the others picked it up and it echoed and repeated and was answered till I nearly went deaf with it all.

I was in a funny mood though, so instead of leaving the room so they'd quiet down, I felt around the walls for a light switch and found one and turned it on.

It wasn't but one bulb, but because it came out of the dark it near to blinded me and the dogs got even louder and thrashed around in their cages. The sound came from everywhere and liked to swallow me up. I walked into the middle of the room and I turned myself around and around and around. All I had in the back of my mind was to break all the cages open and let the dogs go free.

And the noise! They must have heard it on the moon. But suddenly I knew it was from all the dogs smelling me, and that if I let them out they would eat me. Pete said that for training they were hungry.

I got frightened. In my head I saw dogs' cages breaking open, dogs racing each other to be first to get me and then I had to get out.

I left the warehouse the way I came in and I went fast. When I got out I headed back to my nest by walking along the road. Out in the open. No shadows, just panic.

I saw them before they saw me but it was nothing better than blind luck.

They were coming out of the guard's hut and even though I couldn't hear what was being said, I could tell they were angry. Miller slammed the hut door behind him and kicked at it.

Him and Proffitt walked back to the gate. They opened it, walked out, locked the chain, and then I lost sight of them as they headed away from me along the sidewalk.

I used the shadows and made for my nest in the bushes. Then I watched for a while. I didn't understand it, but I worked two things out. One was that I had been right about them maybe checking up on me, though I was wrong about where they'd do it. The other was that if they relocked the chain on the gate it meant they had a key to open it in the first place.

After a while I began to get sleepy, but then I heard chain falling loose again and the gate swinging open. I looked out, and it was Pete walking in! He closed the gate, then he headed down the road towards the warehouse. That was when I couldn't remember turning out the light in the dog room.

I *didn't* follow after him. I kept as still in the bushes as I could. And I fell asleep without seeing him walk back.

12.

What I had arranged for the morning was to meet Proffitt in a laundromat less than a mile from the Fairgrounds hut. The deal was nine o'clock, but I was awake with the first trucks passing by on the road outside the fence which was somewhat after six.

Personal hygiene is tricky in a clump of bushes but outdoors is when I make a bigger effort. I took the time to clean my nails and brush my hair and my jacket, and I folded my good shirt up for its place in my file. I would have planned to do some washing at the laundromat, but Rosie likes me to do it at her place, which makes her feel useful after I've met her and carried her bags.

What I did was leave my sleeping bag in a corner of the hut. If Proffitt said the spying job was finished I could pick it up on the way back to town. If not, it would be there handy when I needed it next, though with Rosie coming in on the two-thirty, she was sure to have her plans for me and a sleeping bag wasn't part of them.

The laundromat was part of an old shopping center and there weren't many people around. There was a doughnut restaurant and that's where I bought myself a good breakfast and finished cleaning up. It still left me plenty of time to scout around before Proffitt was due.

While I was doing that I got the idea for a song, about being cold at night in the city light. I hummed that through to myself three or four times, but I didn't get very far. Still, it was something to work on. Not that it was cold every night yet, but it always pays to think ahead. My long johns were stored under the stairs at Rosie's.

A storage place under the stairs is one of the things I've built for Rosie's house. She likes a place to put things safe, and she also lets me keep just a few of my own things there. Though no way would she ever think about me moving in with her, despite I stay out back sometimes, when the weather's cold and she's at home.

Rosie is a very private and personal woman and she has her own way to do things at her age. She also likes her own independence and that suits us both because I'm the same and I respect it. For instance I wouldn't use her house to sleep in, even though I could get inside, no problem, and it stands empty a lot.

The only time I would consider it would be if I was really sick, but even then I wouldn't use any electricity, because of the principle of the thing and not just because she writes down the meter reading when she goes away, which is an old habit of her husband. But I am not a person that gets sick, though I'm sure she wouldn't mind.

When Proffitt came, he was alone. And he was right on time. He parked and took a bag off the back seat and went into the laundromat.

Through the window I watched him pick out a machine and buy some suds and get some quarters and put his clothes in.

That impressed me, to tell the truth. Other cops I've known never protect guys by making their business meetings look accidental.

To tell the truth, most cops are so full of how they're better than you that they just don't think or don't care, even though it's *you* that has what *they* want. You give him what he wants, but for a thank-you he treats you like you're nothing. It's mostways like being a woman. Women have what men want, but in the end it's the women who get screwed. By Proffitt going through the motions he showed some respect for me, which gave me more respect for him.

He saw me come in through the door. There was a nod and I sat down next to him and he said, "I didn't know if I'd be seeing you this morning, Mr. Moro."

I didn't give him the chance to make the running. I said, "I saw you guys come and check up on me last night. You tell Miller, he keeps kicking doors he's going to hurt his toes."

Proffitt was surprised. "Y'all were there? How come you didn't come out and say hello?"

"You said to keep watch. You didn't say I had to hello everybody."

"We thought you'd be in the hut."

"I went for a walk."

He looked at me.

I said, "I told you I could see things without people seeing me."

"That's true. You did."

"I keep my side of bargains. Do you?"

"I've got your money," he said, and he patted his jacket. Then he looked around the laundromat, but there was only one old woman in the place apart from us, and she was clear the other side. He said, "So what did you see last night, Mr. Moro?"

"A lot," I said.

"I'm listening." He was too. He was paying me close mind.

"After you guys dropped me off I remembered I didn't have my sleeping bag, so I had to go downtown to pick it up."

He said, “We’d have run you back for it.”

“I only remembered after you’d gone, but once I was down there I thought it wouldn’t do any harm to stop at the Linger Longer, just for a minute, to see if I could get my business with Billy Cigar done and out of the way. Well, no sooner was I talking to Billy than he got called away to his office. Naturally he invited me to come along, and who do you think was there?”

“Who?”

“None other than that guy Pete from the dog place, the mean-looking one. Only he was sitting there, nice as you please, along with Linda—that’s Billy’s wife. And this Pete, he had a suit on and he was talking like he’s a human being and not like he eats his own toes.”

“What was he doing there?”

“He was telling Linda, and then Billy, what a terrible business this Cobb guy is doing out at the Fairgrounds, and that’s the first thing I’ve found out for you, what the business is.”

“What’s the business?”

“Cobb trains dogs to fight pigs.” I expected Proffitt to say something to that but he didn’t. I said, “Did you ever hear of dog and hog fighting?”

“Not around here,” he said, which meant he’d heard about it someplace else, but of course he *was* a country boy.

I said, “Another thing, this Cobb microwaved a puppy to death. No lie.”

“That’s not very nice,” Proffitt said.

“But there was something else too.”

“What?”

Carefully I said what I had planned to say. “Pete was there to get Billy to hit Cobb.”

“Hit? You mean kill him?”

“They never said the word, but what Pete wanted was for Billy to put Cobb out of business. Now, how many ways do you know to get a guy like Cobb to pack up when he doesn’t want to?”

“Well, well, well,” Proffitt said.

"A few years ago Billy killed about a hundred people in some South America country, only they can't touch him because the extradition's wrong. A guy like that doesn't send a letter when it comes to taking somebody out of a business."

Proffitt said, "And did Billy Cigar agree to do this hit?"

"When I left, he was talking it over with Linda, but I'm sure Pete made a strong impression."

Proffitt got up. But it wasn't to duck out on me. It was to check how his clothes were doing. When he sat down again I said, "You want to know what I think you guys should do? You and Miller?"

He seemed surprised that I'd offer advice, but the way I figured it I'd had longer to think it all over than he had. And business is business. He said, "What should we do?"

"You guys should give me one of those portable telephones."

"Oh yeah?"

"I know Billy better than you, right? Well if Billy does something about Cobb, he's going to make sure that Pete is out of the way first. So if I have a telephone, I can call you whenever Pete leaves the dog place, and that would be a sign that something might happen out there. If you wanted me to follow Pete for you, you could give me a car too. I can drive. It's no problem. Of course, all this greater responsibility ought to mean some more money, gas for the car and so on."

"Hang on, hang on."

"Am I going too fast for you?"

"I'm going to have to talk to Captain Miller about all this, Mr. Moro," Proffitt said.

"I understand."

"And I wouldn't get your hopes up too high."

"Me, all I'm doing is telling you how it ought to happen. But if there's one true thing about this life, it's that what ought to happen isn't always what does happen."

"You're not wrong there. Mr. Moro."

I leaned towards him. I said, "I've given you stronger information than you ever thought I would, haven't I? I think that's worth a bonus, don't you?"

"I'll talk to Captain Miller about that too, Mr. Moro. But, here, let me give you the twenty-five I still owe you for last night, and another twenty-five on account for tonight." He took out his wallet and counted out five tens. I could see he had more than another hundred in cash in there and I wondered if he'd been planning to pay me off.

But I took the fifty and said, "Thanks." That's basic manners and I try to use them, even with cops.

"Mr. Moro, you sure have given us a lot to think about. Where can I find you this afternoon?"

"I'll call you at your office. Same number, right?" And I recited it for him to show I knew it.

"All right," he said. "Call me this afternoon. And make sure you do it, hear?"

13.

I left while he was moving his clothes to a dryer. Who'd ever have figured a cop for flowers on his underpants?

I still had time to do some business before Rosie came in on the two-thirty bus from Chicago, so I headed for the alleys and backway places I know on the north side. But after a while I found my mind just wasn't on it. My mind was thinking about my business with the cops, so all that happened in the alleys was that I headed towards town.

With cops the usual risk is that you do the work for them and then you don't get paid for it, but so far this time it was easy getting the cash. In the laundromat Proffitt didn't even ask for a receipt. But call me a suspicious so-and-so, something felt wrong and that feeling wouldn't go away.

After I crossed a bridge over Fall Creek I stopped in a bar

and broke one of the tens for a beer. The place was dark, apart from neon light, and it was mostly empty, only the one old guy sitting in the corner. I was about to shift myself and my beer to a solitary table when the bartender started talking to me in a quiet voice.

"You see Chuck over there next to the window?" he said.

"Yeah."

"He had six wives."

"No kidding?" I said. "All at once?"

"No no. One after the last, like that King Henry the Six in England. And, listen up, every one of them wives got a house off him."

I looked over at Chuck. He seemed like an ordinary guy. "He had six houses?" I said.

The bartender had a sip from his own beer. "What happened was whenever he married one of them women, he bought up an old house. Then he fixed it, no leaks, new boiler, the whole shebang. But once him and the woman got comfortable it'd all start to fester, so they'd split the sheet, and each time the woman got the house."

"I'll be," I said.

"A friend of his was talking about it, only a couple of weeks ago," the bartender said. "Chuck don't brag on it hisself. The friend said, 'When there's a warm spring and he ain't already hitched, ol' Chuck gets the urge to go out and give some damn woman a house.' "

I looked over at Ol' Chuck again. He still hadn't moved. Maybe between all the marrying and all the house repairing he needed the rest. I said, "I wonder if Liz Taylor gives them each a house," and I picked up my beer.

But the bartender still wanted to talk. "None of his wives was a lady, you know. Not one."

"No?"

"You know how to tell a lady, don't you?"

"How?"

"She has a bath and don't piss in it. That's how you tell a

lady!" While the bartender was laughing I wondered how he knew so much about Chuck's wives, but I didn't ask. About that time another old guy came in, and I took the moment to move away with my drink. Normally I'd have stayed to listen to some stories, but what I needed was time to sort out my thinking about Billy and what would happen if he decided to shut down Cobb and his dog business.

I picked out a nice dark table. I sipped from my beer.

Billy Cigar was a rough-edged guy, no question about it. And he sure wasn't a guy to get on the wrong side of. But underneath the tough talk I had a hunch about Billy. My hunch was that maybe he had a soft side to him too.

I thought that because in a funny way Billy reminded me of my own daddy, especially the way Daddy was after my momma died and he was hunting around to sort his life out. What I remember best was how sometimes he'd be furious angry and hit us—all three of us and not just me—but later the same night he'd cry on your shoulder and be sorrier than just about any human person I've ever known.

Of course Billy had more breaks in his life than my daddy did, especially the break of meeting Linda who had the great idea for getting rich. What I figured was that Billy maybe kept a soft spot for Linda no matter whose hand he rubbed in the club. So maybe Billy would do things for Linda that were not his own first choice of things to do for himself. That's why I figured Billy would put Cobb out of the dog business, and maybe even out of this world. Linda sure had seemed het up about it, once Pete explained it to her.

But whatever Billy did, Pete would know it was Billy behind it, and that's why I figured Billy would play fair with Pete and warn him. Maybe he'd even do more, even give Pete a job.

And then I realized that Pete wasn't the only guy Billy would have to keep sweet. I'd been there, right? Heard the whole story. So maybe Billy would think he had to square me too.

When I thought of that, it cheered me up a lot. Billy might offer me some job, but maybe what I would take instead was him to finance the clothes deodorant or the smokers' hood. I began to get excited and I made my plan to go back to the Linger Longer Lounge tonight if I possibly could.

There are times that your luck is on a roll, and I thought maybe this was a time like that for me. People talk about lady luck and people talk about making your own luck and it sure is true that you got to work at luck to keep it coming your way. For sure, when your luck is in you got to ride it.

Once I saw how there might be a good opportunity for me even if my business with the cops went bad, I felt better. I downed my beer and headed for town.

On the way to the bus station I stopped for lunch behind a Mexican restaurant and there was plenty to eat and it had good taste. There is an amazing amount of waste in the world, and a lot of it is out back of restaurants.

When I got to the station I took the chance to clean up fresh and then I sat down to wait for Rosie. No way would she want me to spend the night doing business, but there was a good reason for me to go to the Linger Longer. So I had the idea that maybe I should take Rosie to the Linger Longer with me. It wasn't our usual type of place, but I could use some of the cop money and she'd probably like that.

Of course, if when I called Proffitt the cops gave me the car, then maybe I could cover every place I was supposed to be and even get back to the dogs after Rosie went to sleep.

Why I asked Proffitt for the car was because I happen to know there's a law in Indiana that says when a car gets used in a crime and the cops catch it, the car gets confiscated. Considering the number of crimes that take place, the cops must have cars coming out of their ears.

And then I thought maybe, after a good meal and enough drinks, maybe Rosie'd even come back to the dogs with me. She wouldn't like the idea of the bushes, not at her age, but if I didn't spell it out and put it to her right and she came, once we got in there it would be real cosy.

It never once for a minute crossed my mind that the two-thirty bus might come in with Rosie not on it.

14.

The driver said the bus came from Chicago, all right, and he swore he hadn't left early or left anybody behind. And he was sure there was nobody still on board, stuck in a seat or sleeping or dead or anything. I asked him so hard he let me look for myself.

I just didn't know what to do next and my brain was going crazy with it. I'd met Rosie a dozen times and I know for a personal fact that she gets to the bus station about an hour early to be sure she doesn't miss it.

I couldn't think of anything to do but to go to a bar and buy a beer and try to calm down and not pay attention to what my brain was trying to think. But I kept feeling strange and disconnected, and I couldn't concentrate on what people in the bar were talking about.

It wasn't till nearly the end of the afternoon that I remembered I was supposed to call Proffitt and call myself a thousand and one.

He said, "I expected to hear from you earlier, Mr. Moro."

"I forgot," I said.

"You're playing this pretty cool."

"You didn't say I had to call at some special time limit."

"Keep your hair on," he said.

"My hair doesn't fall off. Does yours?"

"Are you all right, Mr. Moro?"

"Never better. Have you got something to say, or should I get on and do my own business?"

"We need to talk," Proffitt said.

"So talk."

"Face-to-face. How long will it take you to get to the laundromat?"

"I don't want to go out there. I'm in town."

"All right. Do y'all want to come over to headquarters? I'll wait for you by the entrance."

"I don't want to go there either."

"Well where then, for Christ's sake?"

"Let's make it the Hilton," I said.

"What?"

"Don't you know the Hilton Hotel, Homer? It's on the corner of Meridian Street and Ohio."

While I was waiting for Proffitt I remembered a story about a cop and Ohio Street. A guy told it in a bar I was in once. He was old himself and he was talking about his big brother, who was a cop back in the thirties.

The brother was walking his beat one day when he turned the corner onto Massachusetts Avenue and found a dead horse.

The horse was just lying there. It wasn't connected to a milk wagon, or a cart or anything. It didn't even have a bridle. But it was dead for sure, and it was lying in the gutter and there wasn't anything to do but arrange for it to be picked up and towed away.

But the first thing the brother did was grab the horse by the back legs. And he dragged the horse around the corner.

"Why did he do that?" everybody in the bar asked the guy telling the story.

"Because," the guy said, "my brother knew he'd have to write a report, and he could spell Ohio but he sure couldn't spell Massachusetts."

Big hotels are good places. As long as you're not totally dirty you can just walk in and sit in the lobby. All you've got to do is act like you belong there and pick a time they're busy with people checking in and going out, when the guys that work there are jumping around to make tips. Come midnight, someone would notice and throw you out, but if you're careful they can be a good place to warm up or use the john. Hotels aren't all the same, but I find the Hilton comfortable and suitable to my needs. It also has a way to walk to the lobby that you don't have to pass the front desk.

Proffitt didn't take long. I saw him before he saw me so I stood up and stuck out my hand for a shake and said, "Homer, great to see you!"

I talked loud, which was part of the act, but when he got close and said, "You've got some nerve, Moro," it was hardly a whisper.

"Business is all about taking risks," I said. I heard that on television once and it stuck in my mind. Then I said, "I'm starving. Are you going to buy me something to eat?"

He hesitated, but I didn't care. I just headed for the bar.

We sat by a low wall with plants growing out of it, away from the street windows which is where the other customers were. A waiter asked what we wanted. I said a sandwich and a beer, and then I said, "Is that all right?" to Proffitt, to make sure that the waiter knew who was paying.

When the waiter went away, Proffitt said, "Are you sure

you feel O.K., Mr. Moro? Your face is flushed and you're jumping around like a hot twitchet."

"I'm all right," I said. "Just looking forward to having a car to do all that good work for you guys with."

Proffitt gave his head one quick shake and he narrowed up his eyes, but then he said, "Captain Miller and I went through everything you told me this morning."

"Yeah?"

"And there's been a change of plan."

"What do you mean a change of plan? I come up with good stuff you didn't know so you're going to try to weasel out of the money you owe me?"

"The financial arrangements remain the same," Proffitt said.

"I bet."

"You going to hear me out?"

I didn't say I would, but I didn't say I wouldn't.

Proffitt said, "Yesterday we didn't know what goes on at the Fairgrounds. Now we do."

"Because of what I found out," I said.

"So what Miller and I want you to do is keep an eye on Billy Sigra tonight."

"An eye? You mean, at his club?"

"That's right. We want to know who he talks to, and when he's there. But he mustn't know you're watching him and if he leaves, don't follow. Do you think you can do that?"

The man wanted to pay me to do what I wanted to do anyway! But I still sucked some air and made a face. "I don't know," I said. "It's a lot riskier because I won't have anyplace dark to hide. You ought to give me more money."

"We'll give you expense money to spend in the club."

"How much?"

"Thirty bucks ought to see you through the night if you don't go buying champagne and women."

"I'll need at least sixty," I said.

"Call it fifty," Proffitt said.

"No, Homer, sixty is what I'll need and sixty's what I've got to have." I was in a funny old mood.

"All right, all right," Proffitt said. But he wasn't very happy about it.

I said, "What did Miller decide about the bonus for my information being so good?"

"He said he'd take it into account when the job was over."

"That's no good, Homer."

Proffitt looked at me hard. He said, "Captain Miller did *not* like the fact that you went back to the Linger Longer when you'd been told to stay put out with the dogs."

"I told you, I had to get my sleeping bag."

Proffitt looked around the room, and at the same time he leaned right over the table. When he turned back to me, he grabbed a handful of my shirt and we were nose to nose. He said, "I've had enough of you jerking me around, *Jan*. And I'm telling you, from here on in you have two ways to go, only two."

"Let go of me!"

"You can do what we tell you to do, and consider yourself lucky, because that's what you fucking are."

"Yeah?"

"Or you can get locked up."

"Locked up? In jail?"

"Hole in one."

"That's not fair!"

"Fuck fair, *Jan*. And I'll tell you something else for nothing. If it was up to Miller you'd have been locked up from the start."

I said, "All I did was come to the cops like a good citizen is supposed to and now you're threatening to put me in jail!"

"Stop shouting, for Christ's sake." He let me go.

"I don't *want* to go back to jail!"

He said, "You've been inside before? It's not on your record."

"It wasn't in this state." And then I didn't say anything more, because the time I spent in jail was not a good time.

Funny things happened to my head in there and I didn't want to go through that again. Which is one of the reasons I'm just a businessman now and I don't do anybody any harm.

Proffitt said, "I don't want to give you any trouble, Mr. Moro. But you're going to have to do what we tell you to do. Play it that way and you'll stay out of jail and you'll make some money."

I didn't say anything.

The waiter brought my sandwich and my beer. I went for the beer first, and it tasted good. And then I got the germ of an idea. I said, "You guys haven't told me the whole story about what you're doing."

"We haven't?"

I said, "No way is all this happening just because you told Miller what I said about the dogs and he felt sorry for them."

Proffitt was quiet first, then he laughed like he couldn't keep it in. It was as if he was suddenly friendly and not like a cop at all. "Miller hates goddamn dogs," he said.

"Sergeant Proffitt, what *is* going on?"

He didn't say anything and I started on the sandwich. When I finished it he was looking at me different, like for the first time he was seeing me as a human person. He said, "I've run a lot of informants over the years, but I don't know how to figure you."

"Maybe it's because I'm not not as stupid as you think, even though I'm a little down on my luck."

"That could be," he said. "But I'll tell you this, Jan Moro, or whatever your name is, you've stumbled into something that's bigger than you can handle and you'll either come out of it with some cash or you'll come out of it with nothing but grief."

"There is one way," I said, "that I'll do whatever you want me to and I'll do it for nothing."

That surprised him.

I said, "To tell you the truth, Sergeant Proffitt, I need a favor."

"What favor?"

"I've got a friend," I said. "She should have been on a bus today, only she wasn't."

"Yeah?"

"Can you find out what happened to her?"

There it was. The idea. Cops have a whole department for missing people. If anybody could find out what happened to Rosie, they could.

15.

After Proffitt left, I went all shaky. Getting too worked up isn't a good thing for me which I know from experience. I had to get outdoors to try to calm down. I decided to walk around the alleys for a while, with the plan of ending up at the bus station in forty-five minutes, which was when I was supposed to call Proffitt at his office.

But instead of the alleys what happened was that I went into a store and I bought a new shirt. I can't hardly remember when I ever did that before.

This shirt was cotton, a gray that looked metallic, and it had a white collar and cuffs and it came with a pure white tie. It cost over twenty dollars, with tax, and I was so surprised at what I was doing that when I paid the money over I giggled when the clerk gave me the change. I don't know what got into me.

I went straight over to the bus station and put the shirt on and the tie, and I felt teary, I looked so good in the mirror.

The last fifteen minutes waiting I spent on a bench. An old woman came up and asked if she could help, and I truly said she couldn't.

When I called Proffitt, he said, "There's no Jane Does in the Chicago morgue that sound like your Rosie, and no Rose Goody on the dead list. But I talked to a real good friend of mine in the Missing Persons here in town. They have all the contacts there to find things out. You call 923-5338 and ask for Sergeant Fleetwood and mention my name. You got a pen for the number?"

"I remember it," I said. "923-5338."

"O.K. Then you call me in the morning, hear?"

I felt teary again for a minute, because Proffitt was talking to me like I was someone he knew.

I called Sergeant Fleetwood, who turned out to be a woman sergeant. She said, "I was expecting your call, Mr. Moro. Homer Proffitt says you've got a friend you're concerned about."

"I sure am."

"Well, I'll help you in any way I can. Maybe you could fill me in on the facts."

I told Sergeant Fleetwood everything I knew about Rosie and Tulip and the rest of Rosie's family and how Rosie never missed a bus in her life.

"That's fine," Sergeant Fleetwood said. "That gives us a good start."

"If there's anything *I* can do to help you out with this, you just got to say."

"I'll take it for the time being," she said. "See what I can find out."

"You sure?"

"The only thing is could you let me know right away if Rosie turns up at home, or you hear anything else about her."

"I'll go up and check her house right now," I said. She gave me a number to leave messages on if I found anything out and we hung up. I headed for Rosie's house.

On the way while I was walking I thought about how it would be a shame if Rosie didn't get to see me in my shirt when it was new. Even though probably what would happen was that she would tease me about it.

And that reminded me of this story I heard in a bar once, about Giovanni the Sheep Shagger. This guy Giovanni, he was known all over Italy as Giovanni the Sheep Shagger. He was famous so one of the newspapers sent a reporter to the village where Giovanni lived. The reporter found Giovanni's house and knocked on the door and when Giovanni answered the reporter said to him, "Let's go straight for it, man. All of Italy wants to know. *Why* are you called Giovanni the Sheep Shagger?"

And Giovanni says, "I've lived all my life in this one village. All my life. And I do wonderful things here. I bake great bread, great! And I do that every morning. But do people call me Giovanni the Baker? No! And, I build strong, solid houses. Everybody wants one. And I do that in the afternoon. But do people call me Giovanni the House Builder? No! And, I paint beautiful pictures, oil pictures. And people pay me money to paint pictures for them. But do people call me Giovanni the Painter? Never! And my poems. Lovers all over the village want my poems. Giovanni the Poet? No no! But, I go out and shag one little sheep . . . !"

Rosie would have called me Jan the Shirt Buyer forever more. For one little shirt. That's life for you.

When I got to Rosie's house it was totally dark and locked up. But instead of looking at the house and being sad, I turned right around and headed back to town. No point in assuming the worst till Sergeant Fleetwood had a chance to get all the facts.

And then, when I realized what was happening, I stopped on the sidewalk. I stood like a statue, just about in the middle of a step, because my whole life was turning on its head. I was trusting cops now.

16.

I got to the Linger Longer about nine. I went straight to the front door, ready to tip Ed one of Proffitt's sixty bucks, but the guy on the door wasn't Ed. This was a smaller guy that the doorman suit looked baggy on, and he rocked from foot to foot and seemed restless and not happy to be outside the club at all. Still, he didn't give me any trouble about going in, which shows what a new shirt'll do.

Even though it was a Friday, there weren't many people inside and I couldn't see Billy anyplace. But I was at the Linger Longer on business and it was my job to stay there, so I went to the horseshoe bar and ordered a tequila sunrise. My mood was light from not having to worry about Rosie till tomorrow. I gave the bartender a twenty and when he passed back the change, I asked if Billy was around.

First he said, "No." Then he said, "Hey, you're the little

guy was in here last night, aren't you?" And even before I decided what to say, he was waving to one of the bouncers.

So I said, "Yeah, that's me. Billy and me have some business."

The bouncer who came over was no one I had ever seen before. He said, "You Starch?"

I said, "What?" but he took that for a yes.

"Billy said if you come in you gotta talk to Linda."

I was amazed. Billy Cigar left word about *me*?

"I'll talk to Linda," I said. "Happy to."

The bouncer said, "This way."

And I said, "O.K. Great. Lead on, MacDowell," and we headed off across the lounge just like the night before with Billy. I could only guess that it had something to do with Pete and the dogs and maybe about how to keep me sweet.

We went through the combination door and I said, "If Linda's in the office, I know my way," but the bouncer kept leading me anyhow.

When we got to the office he stopped and said, "Spread, will ya? I gotta pat ya down." I leaned against a wall and he did a thorough job and even checked I didn't have a knife in my socks and then he turned to the door and he knocked, and waited.

A voice inside said, "Yeah," and the bouncer opened the door and sent me in. Linda Cigar was alone and she was standing in the middle of the room.

Even though last time I was so distracted seeing Pete, I remembered Linda was elegant and red-headed. But on top of that she looked like an athlete, the way she stood. It said that she could take care of herself and that she wouldn't depend for anything on anybody, except maybe for Billy.

"Ah, little Starch," she said. "Come in. Sit down."

I looked over my shoulder, like she was talking to somebody else. When I thought I'd made the point I said, "Do you mean me? 'Cause if so, my name's Jan Moro." And I stuck out my hand.

But she didn't shake it or move or do anything except say, "I have been told that your name is Clarence Starch, Junior."

"Who said that?"

"A person who knew you in Detroit."

I couldn't remember seeing anybody I knew last night but I said, "Detroit? Well, that explains it. Up there I used the name Clarence Starch for a while, but now I've gone back to Jan Moro."

"So, you just used the name, and your father is not also Clarence Starch?"

That one caught me, because I don't like to deny my own daddy. I always thought that, by now, no one remembered him. Even so, I tried to keep my options open by saying, "My daddy's been gone for a long time, Mrs. Cigar."

"Is he not still in the Pendleton Prison?"

Well, she had caught me out and she knew it. But instead of worrying about it, I was feeling sad because of the long time since I'd been to visit Daddy. I think about him a lot and I try to learn from his mistakes, but it wasn't until that very moment I realized how upset I'd be if Daddy died before I saw him again. I resolved to go visit him the next chance I got, even though it's always a hard thing to say the right things when you're visiting in a prison.

I know that from what guys said where I was. They were forever coming back from a visit and saying how they wished they'd have said this or said that but they didn't think of it in time. Probably the people that visited them felt the same too.

My daddy's locked away because he killed a cop. It didn't happen like they said in court, but it did happen and that's how it is. I don't advertise it anymore because people get the wrong idea about me. Maybe it used to be the right idea, but now I'm more mature and I stay away from the rough stuff and try to use my head. Singers and TV actors change their name for business. Why not me? No big deal about that.

"What?"

Linda said, "I told you to sit down, Mr. Starch."

"Sorry." I sat, but I wasn't comfortable. I'd have been all right talking to Billy, but Linda was a whole different kettle of fish. I couldn't see how there would ever be a way for me to do anything for her that she'd like.

Linda said, "You want a drink?"

"I'll have a beer, thanks."

She opened me a bottle of beer and she poured it into a glass. The beer tasted good and it helped me settle down. I said, "Good beer, Mrs. Cigar."

She sat down facing me. She said, "Do you have a line of work, Mr. Starch?"

"I'm in business for myself," I said. "In fact, I had a business idea that I wanted to tell your husband about, which is why I'm back around the club tonight. Is Mr. Cigar around?"

"Billy does not remember meeting you before last night."

"It was in a bar once where he bought drinks for the house. And can I just say how everybody in the place said what a nice guy Mr. Cigar is, and how he tells the story about South America and what a great idea you had and how much he owes to you."

She thought about that and then she said, slowly, "Do men in the bar also speak of Billy's temper?"

"No, ma'am, I never heard that."

"Because my Billy has a most terrible temper, Mr. Starch."

"Yeah?"

"And do you know what makes him get so angry?"

"No, ma'am, I don't."

"It is when a person says the wrong things to the wrong people."

We sat looking at each other for a minute.

She said, "Do you understand me, Mr. Starch?"

"I believe I do," I said. She was warning me off with a threat.

"Do you remember meeting a Mr. Pete Yount here last night?"

"No, ma'am," I said. "I certainly do not."

She laughed at that. And she liked it, that I picked up her drift so quick and was acting scared of her.

"Yount says that he first met you at the very place in the Fairgrounds where he works for the awful man with the dogs."

I said, "If I try real real hard I can bring the memory back for just a fleeting second."

"Well, Mr. Starch, Billy and I want to know what it was that you were doing in the Fairgrounds when Yount met you."

"Mrs. Cigar, I'll tell you the truth. Sometimes I have trouble finding a place to sleep at night. Out at the Fairgrounds they have empty buildings and they can be handy for a night or two."

"You looked for a place to sleep?"

"Yes, ma'am. But, since meeting Mr. Yount, I've found myself a nice place to sleep that's entirely on the other side of town and I'll be able to sleep there regularly, from now on."

"That is fortunate for you I think."

"Yeah, I got lucky," I said.

We were both quiet after that till she said, "You will do well to remember what I have said about Billy and his temper."

"I will. I have a real good memory," I said. "For some things."

"You may go now, Mr. Starch."

I stood up, but instead of leaving right away I said, "I just want you to know, Mrs. Cigar, that I am a deep animal lover myself. And anybody who loves animals as much as you do is O.K. by me."

17.

I walked back into the lounge and as soon as I got there I could see guys all over the place were looking at me, the bartender and the bouncer and a couple of others. Normally I don't get noticed, so I guess they knew I was in with Linda and maybe didn't think I'd get out alive.

I gave them a little wave and I walked back across to where I'd been at the bar. The bartender brought my tequila sunrise up and the level was right where I left it. I hopped on a stool and took a sip.

There was already more of a crowd than before, and I took a look around for somebody I knew from Detroit, but I didn't see anyone. Then I leaned my elbows on the bar, and I enjoyed just how good it felt to begin to relax. I sipped some more from my drink.

Then, somebody tapped me on the shoulder.

I spun around and I was amazed to see it was the loose girl from the threesome the night before, the girl who'd made a play for Billy. She stood there in a shiny blue dress that was cut low at the top and cut high at the bottom and she gave me a moment to take it in before she said, "Excuse me."

"Yeah?"

"Don't get the wrong idea but can I buy you a drink?"

"Uh, thanks, but I've already got one."

She shifted her weight from one leg to the other, which made a rustling sound, and she sighed and she said, "There's no house limit, you know."

She bought me another tequila sunrise and had a daiquiri for herself. We moved from the bar to a little table nearby. This woman was about thirty and very clean and neat with a lot of makeup and I could tell that guys around the room were watching me again.

Most of the men in the place would have been happy for a woman like that to buy them a drink. I wasn't unhappy—a free drink doesn't cost anything—but I knew that for her to buy me a drink, out of everybody in the place, there had to be a particular reason.

"Thanks for the drink," I said. "What's your name?"

"Call me Barb."

"Hi, Barb."

"Hi. And what's your name?"

"Jan."

"Hi. Oh, I already said hi." She giggled like a little girl.

"Yeah, you did," I said.

"I hope you don't think that I buy a drink for every man I meet, Jan."

"I don't think that, Barb," I said.

"Good."

"I think you only buy men tequila sunrises who you want something from."

For a tiny moment she was surprised. She laughed, and

although it was only a little laugh, it wasn't anything like the giggle.

"Don't feel you have to hurry saying what you want," I said. "You can buy me drinks the rest of the night if you want to."

She didn't laugh this time but she said, "You're funny," and it was a compliment.

"I'm going to have my own TV show one day," I said.

"Yeah?"

"Public access."

And she laughed again. Maybe when I get my show I should tell jokes as well as singing my songs.

Barb said, "To tell you the truth, Jan, I picked you out because last night you were with Billy Sigra."

"Yeah," I said. "I was."

"Are you a pal of his?"

"What you saw is what we are."

"You looked like pals. You went off with him."

"You were invited too."

"To see his wife?" she said. "I don't need *that* kind of complication. No way."

"I've just come out from seeing her again tonight," I said.

"You and her got something going?"

"It's strictly business."

She raised her eyebrows at that, but then said, "So, what's she like?"

"Who?"

"Linda's her name, isn't it?"

"Yeah."

"Well?"

"She's a strong person, I think."

"Attractive?"

"Oh yeah."

"More than me?"

Barb wasn't coy about asking that at all. She looked me

straight in the eyes. So I said, "Not more. Different. More glamorous where you're more pretty."

She nodded like she was thinking. She said, "I wouldn't want to look like a wife anyway."

I said, "I thought Billy seemed interested."

"You saw that, huh?"

"But he's not here now."

"So I'm told."

I said, "And even though he's not here, you're waiting? You got a thing about Billy? Is that it?"

"That's one way to describe it. Yeah," she said. "I have *got* to see that man." When I didn't say anything to that right away she said, "You're shocked, aren't you?"

"No."

"What then?"

"Look," I said, "I don't understand why you're telling me all this."

"It's because you're Billy's friend. The bartender won't tell me where he is. The bouncer won't tell me where he is. I want you to tell me where he is."

"Sorry. I don't know."

"For real? Or are you just protecting him?"

I laughed at that.

But Barb said, "It's not funny, you prick."

"I wasn't laughing at you. Just the idea that Billy Cigar would need me to protect him."

"Yeah. All right. Sorry, I guess."

Then I got an idea. I said, "Hey, what about that guy you were with last night?"

"Ramón? What about him?"

"He knew Billy to talk to. Maybe he knows where Billy is."

"Ramón doesn't know."

"You sure?"

"Yeah, I'm sure."

"Oh."

"So, you don't know where Billy is?"

"Nope. I asked for him myself. He's not around and nobody could say when he'll be back."

"But he'll come here tonight?"

"I don't know."

"That's straight?"

"I've got no reason to lie to you, Barb."

"I've heard *that* before, only about a million times," she said. She looked at me again but then she said, "O.K. I believe you."

"So what are you going to do?"

"Wait here, I guess. What else can I do?"

"I don't know," I said.

"You waiting for him too?"

"Well, I guess I am," I said.

"Is it O.K. if I wait with you? It'll keep guys from hitting on me. I'll buy all the drinks. But don't expect anything else."

"Are you rich or something?"

"Oh yeah! I'd really be here doing this if I was an heiress." She laughed loud but short. "No, Jan, I'm not rich. But I do have a kind of allowance. Sounds like I'm a kid, doesn't it? Second childhood. I guess that's what comes after growing up the first time."

"I'm not going to drink much," I said. "But would your allowance run to buying me something to eat?"

After Barb got another daiquiri we moved to the restaurant part of the lounge. When a waiter came over, Barb told him, "Give this man anything he wants."

The waiter wanted to show me a menu but I didn't look at it. "A steak and fries and a big salad and chocolate ice cream," I said. "If that's O.K."

"Anything, Jan, really." Then she told the waiter to keep the daiquiris coming.

While I ate, Barb drank. I asked her about her life and she told me how she grew up in country Indiana but wanted to be an actress so she spent some time in Chicago and then in New York before giving up. In New York she got involved with a Mexican and down there she met a government official from Guatemala and spent three years with him before she quit that and came back to Indy. "I learned a lot down there," she said, "and all of it in Spanish."

She didn't come from Indy to begin with. "Daddy was a farmhand down near Hanover, but I used to say 'I come from French Lick,' and I'd open my eyes wide like I didn't know what I was saying. People in New York thought that was funny. You sure do grow up fast in places like New York."

Since my own daddy was a farmhand too, in his early life, Barb got to feeling that we had a lot in common and she talked to me about as easy as if I was family, and told me what happened to her brother, who her sisters married, and how her momma died from choking on a chicken bone.

About the only story with a bird and bones in it that I knew to tell back wasn't about a chicken at all but was a story a guy told me in a bar one time and he swore it was true and happened to him.

This guy was living in a town in the south part of the state called Little Acre and he got up one morning and found a baby crow out in his front yard and it had a broken wing. A lot of guys don't like crows but this guy gathered the little crow up and took it to the vet and had the wing set and then he took care of the little crow till it was ready to go back to the wild.

Only as it got better and bigger, the little crow didn't seem to have any inclination at all to leave the comforts of a home in Little Acre, Indiana. And what happened was that the little crow got so tame that everywhere the guy went, the little crow followed after him.

"After a while," the guy said, "I knew it was time for that little crow to spread his wings and fly away, but the danged thing ain't even learned how to fly. So, I set about teachin' him. But how the hell do you teach a goddamn bird how to fly?"

The guy tried just about everything he could think of, but

finally he decided to use the fact that the little crow would follow him anywhere. What the guy did was climb up to the roof of his garage. And the little crow followed him, sure enough.

The guy's idea was, if he jumped off the roof of his garage, then the little crow will do the same, but where the guy will land on the driveway nature would make the crow spread his wings and fly.

So the guy jumped off the roof of his garage.

And so did the little crow.

And what happened was that the both of them each broke a leg.

"This is a true story," the guy said. "It really is. We both broke a goddamned leg."

"Well, what happened to the little crow?" I asked him, because, for sure, the little crow hadn't followed him into the bar we were sitting in.

"We both got better from our broken legs and I got used to the idea that I had me a crow for life," the guy said. "But then one day my Uncle Fredrick from Minnesota was passing through and he stopped by and he was just about the most near-sighted man I ever knew. My Uncle Fredrick sat down on a chair in my living room and that was the end of my little crow."

The best story Barb told me was about a short guy out in the country where she grew up. He was arrested for making love to a farmer's girl and they were supposed to have done it standing up, leaning on the door of a cow barn. But the girl was over six feet tall and the boy was even shorter than me so when the case came to court, the Justice of the Peace set about to work out how the boy and the farmer's girl could have done it at all.

First he thought it was with the boy standing on a bucket, but he went through the barn and made the boy stand on the biggest milk bucket he could find and there was still no way that boy could have got at it without jumping.

In the end the boy was turned loose for lack of evidence.

"But I found out after how they did it," Barb said. "You want to know how?"

"How?"

"The gal told me herself. What they did was put the bucket on her head and then the little guy just hung on to the handle like a flicker."

18.

Barb called it quits at one-thirty in the morning. Billy had still not showed up, and we only stayed that long because she was relaxed and enjoying telling stories about her life. I know that because she said, "Men ask about you sometimes, but they don't really want to know. It's been so long since I told about my momma that sometimes I think I sprung full-growed out of a magazine."

"The staples must have hurt a bundle," I said, and after a moment of looking at me she said, "No, the bundle came through without a scratch," and she laughed like to make it rain, which was probably a lot from the daiquiris. Then she said, "Fuck, we stay here much longer I'll forget what I'm supposed to do anyhow."

"Sounds like a good time to leave," I said.

"Yup," she said, and she stood up. And then she sat down again. "Whoo-ee. I better take that a bit slower."

We had cups of coffee and Barb paid the bill before she stood up again. Her first steps were a little unsteady, but by the time we got out on the sidewalk she was moving pretty well. She said, "Jan Moro, I came back to this godforsaken armpit a year ago and I've had more fun tonight than I've had with a man since. Thank you kindly."

"I had a good time too," I said.

I'm not sure she heard right because she said, "Not tonight. Things are complicated at my place and I probably wouldn't be worth it anyhow." And she began to walk along the street.

I walked along with her. Before we got to the corner, Barb stopped, and to give her credit she didn't lean on anything. "Which way you going, little Jan?"

"I thought I'd walk you home, make sure you get there safe."

"Oh yeah?" She squinted her eyes down at me. "You don't need to do that. I got my car."

"Right. I'll walk you to that."

Her car was about a block away but even in that distance she got steadier, so I figured she'd be all right to get home. She unlocked a nice little light-colored sedan and I held the door as she got in. It took a minute for her to start it up, but she did and then I stood back and waved as she began to drive away.

But she only drove a few yards. I ran after her and bent down at the window. "Something wrong?"

"Look, you want me to drop you somewhere?"

"If you wouldn't mind."

"Why the hell didn't you ask?"

"You bought all the drinks," I said.

"You are just about the strangest little man I ever knowed," she said. "Well, are you getting in or you going to stand there grinning all night?"

I got in.

"Where to?" she asked.

"My stuff's out at the back side of the Fairgrounds. Maybe you won't want to go that far."

"I can get to the goddamn Fairgrounds."

"Well, if we pick my things up and then you drop me somewhere on your way back, that'd be great."

I had Barb stop next to the bushes where the hole in the fence was. She didn't look very happy about it though. "Where *is* this?" she said.

"I go in through the fence there. It's a shortcut."

"How long you going to be? I got to pee."

Inside the fence I was careful to keep to the shadows. I couldn't see anything going on, but Linda Cigar had made me nervous about the Fairgrounds. Billy not being around the club could mean that whatever they were planning was already happening.

But I got to the guard's hut without any problems and it was only a minute to get in, pick up my sleeping bag, and get back out. But sometimes a minute can be too long, because right then, as I was closing the door, I heard voices.

I stopped still, but they weren't more than forty feet away. And facing right at me.

They saw me.

They shouted.

They ran towards me.

I couldn't believe it.

But when guys run at you, legs have a mind of their own. I ran too, back the way I'd come.

Barb was still there. She saw me worm through the fence and she started the car. I jumped in and slammed the door and said, "Let's go, let's go!"

She pulled away all right, but she said, "I know I said I had to pee, but I'm not *that* desperate."

Neither of us spoke for a couple of blocks, but I looked

back a couple of times and then Barb said, "Did something happen?"

I didn't answer at first.

"Jan?"

"A couple of guys chased me."

"Did you thieve something from them?"

"No."

She stopped for a red light. "They guys you know?"

"One of them only has seven toes and he works for a guy who microwaves puppies to death and trains dogs to fight pigs."

She looked at me like I was crazy.

"And the other one is a police captain."

"A what?"

"You heard me."

"Jan, are you in trouble?"

"I don't rightly know," I said.

The light changed and she drove on, but in the middle of the block she pulled over. She said, "Because if you're in trouble and if you really need somewhere to stay, I guess you can stay at my place."

"I don't know how bad the trouble is," I said, "but I sure could use a place to sleep."

She got us rolling again. "I'm going to have to make a phone call," she said.

"A phone call?"

"You deaf as well as short?"

She stopped by the next public phone and she stayed there quite a while. When she hung up and got back in the car she was more relaxed again.

"Is there a problem?" I asked.

"No."

"Because I can pay for a room. I have money."

"Now he tells me," she said. She sighed and then she turned to me and waved a finger. "You may have money, big boy, but no tricks now."

She laughed and started driving again.

* * *

Barb's house was on a little development off a street I knew because it was near Spades Park and it was a little box-shaped house with a yard around it and it had its own driveway, but no garage.

She left the car in the driveway but it took her a while to find the right key for the front door. When we walked in and she turned the light on, she said, "Sorry about the mess."

I didn't see any mess, but I said, "No problem."

She said, "Wait here," and she left me.

Where I waited was a living room, but there wasn't much to furnish it, no rug, and only a table against a wall, a little couch, and a couple of straight-backed chairs. Not even a TV.

But what the room did have was a lot of pictures of Billy Cigar. Propped up on the table was a bulletin board with four snapshots of Billy pinned to it. Lying flat there were newspaper articles and some of them had pictures of Billy too.

When Barb came back she saw me looking at her Billy pictures. I said, "You've got it bad, huh?"

She started putting everything away into a folder.

"I don't butt into other people's business," I said, but she went on putting the stuff away, even the pictures that were pinned up.

Then she said, "Are you any good with plumbing?"

"There a problem?"

"Sometimes I can't get the goddamned toilet to flush. If I don't get it just right the first time, then there's nothing I can do to make it up."

"Show me where," I said.

She led me to the bathroom. It didn't take any fixing. There was nothing wrong, only a handle that had its own quirk that to make it work you had to pump it a couple of times. There are a lot like that around, only you get used to living with them because it's expensive to change a whole john just for a flush.

When I came out I said, "All clear."

"Great. Thanks."

I loosened the strap around my sleeping bag. "Is on the couch all right or would you rather me on the floor?"

"Couch is fine."

"Thanks for letting me stay," I said.

"You want a drink? Or something to eat?"

"No, thanks."

"I don't bring just anybody back here, you know, but you seemed so shook up."

I nodded and I said, "Thank you."

She left me and I guess she went to her bedroom.

She was right about me being shook up. Pete and Miller together. In the middle of the night. Out near the dogs. I only got a glance, but they were talking together like they were friends. How could that be right?

I turned off the lights and got into my sleeping bag. But I couldn't stop thinking about it.

Did Miller catch Pete out there?

Or was Miller crooked, somehow working for Cobb?

I couldn't figure any of it out at all. Except that I knew it wouldn't be good for me.

And I knew I'd never get to sleep.

19.

When I woke up I forgot where I was and whether I was safe. I made like a crawdad to where the couch arm meets the couch back, and I pulled the sleeping bag up around me. It wasn't till then that I saw Barb sitting on the floor, watching me. And I remembered where I was.

I said, "Hi."

She said, "You're a funny one, Jan Moro."

"I am?"

And I had the feeling she was going to say something else, but instead the telephone rang.

She had to get up to answer it. She said, "Hello?" And then, "What time is this to call me? You know how late I was up."

The person on the other end said some more and Barb

looked out a window towards the street. I looked at my watch. It was a few minutes past eight.

Barb said, *"El no estaba allí y eso es todo. Oye, párate. Espera un momento."* Then she covered the phone with her hand and said, "Jan, y'all go into the bathroom for a while, O.K.?"

I got up with the sleeping bag still around me because that was quicker than putting on my outside clothes. Barb was talking again before I got to the bathroom. She said, *"Te dije anoche, Ramón, es un amigo de Billy. He probado a todos los demás. No puedo joder el cabrón si no puedo encontrarlo."*

In the bathroom I didn't know whether to run water to make sure not to hear any more or just to keep quiet as I could. But even without trying I could hear her say, *"¡Claro por eso está aquí!"*

I know enough Spanish to catch a bus, but not enough to understand what Barb was saying, except to know that she called the guy she was talking to Ramón. But since she had me go out of the room even when she was talking Spanish, I put my hands over my ears and hummed one of my own songs. I didn't hear anything more that she said, except I could tell that once she shouted at him. In fact I didn't even know when the call was over because the next thing I heard was Barb knocking on the bathroom door and saying, "You can come out now."

So I went out. I said, "You all right?"

"Nope," she said. And then, when she saw that made me worried, she said, "Yeah, of course I'm all right, asshole."

I didn't know what she meant but I said, "Do you want me to make myself scarce now?"

"Why don't you take a shower and I'll make some breakfast."

I spent a long time in the shower. When Rosie's away, I don't get the chance very often, and it felt real good.

Poor old Rosie. I sure hoped she was O.K., and I would've started worrying over what happened to her except suddenly I got an idea of something to do about Pete and Miller. It was when the hot water first hit my head.

My idea was that no matter what Pete and Miller were up to last night, Billy Cigar would want to know about it. Especially that Pete was out there with a cop. And, if *I* was the one to tell him, Billy would owe me a favor for sure. Maybe a big one!

Working all that out cheered me up and I started singing from another one of my songs.

Maybe what I should do with Billy wasn't talk about the deodorant that you sprayed onto clothes at all, or even the hood for smokers. Maybe the right thing was to get him to sponsor my TV program. I already knew he was interested in music. All he'd have to do was put up the cash and I could do the rest.

I sang louder.

"You sounded happy," Barb said when I got to the kitchen.

"I try to see the bright side of things," I said. And I do. It's part of my business philosophy and helps me to recognize opportunities.

Barb made flapjacks for breakfast, and she served them dripping with butter and syrup. They tasted so good, and I felt so clean, that right in the middle of a mouthful I closed my eyes and began to cry.

My momma loved flapjacks. The smell of them at Barb's made me see Momma's flapjacks cooking in the big iron skillet that she only ever cleaned with salt. I used to stand on a chair to see the bubbles go from filling in again to leaving a hole. Enough holes meant they had to be turned over. I'd call out and Momma would come to the stove and it wouldn't be long then because the second side never got cooked even a minute.

Sometimes Momma made little flapjacks, from just one spoon of batter, and she called them silver dollars and she'd put a big stack of them on a plate and say, "Don't you spend them all at once," and it was a good joke every single time.

And then I remembered, for about the first time, that the day after Momma died, but before the night when Daddy got home, I made some flapjacks for Cissy and Wayne. None of us went to school that day and after a while we got to being hungry. I figured I had watched Momma cook flapjacks so many times I could do it myself, with the flour and the milk and the egg. I tried as hard as I could but they weren't even close to being like Momma's and we all knew it. And then I forgot to turn the stove off under the big pan and the kitchen got all smoky.

"What?"

"Jan?" Barb stood behind me and put her hand on my shoulder and put her face down near mine, and that just made it worse because it made it even better. "What's wrong, honey?"

"Nothing," I said. And I wasn't lying.

When I have a spell living outdoors I get used to things being rough and it doesn't bother me. But a night on a couch, waking up warm, having a shower, eating cooked food and then someone's breath on my neck, it just churned me into butter. It was like I was sponsored already.

"Jan, you sure you're all right?"

"Yeah."

I don't know what Barb thought, but she went back to her chair and sat down and started eating again.

After a while I said, "Good food."

Barb made coffee too and I made her drink it in the living room while I washed up the dishes. Standing at the sink and doing something with my hands brought me back to myself and when I was done I brought my own coffee through and sat with her on the couch.

"We've got to make some plans," she said.

"O.K."

"I'd like to help you out, Jan, I really would, but I just can't let you stay on here."

"Don't worry about mc," I said.

"You're in bad trouble, aren't you?"

"I'm into something, but I don't know whether it's trouble or not. The guys I'm doing business with never tell me the whole truth."

"I sure know that tune backwards," she said.

"But you've got troubles of your own, haven't you?"

"Naw, I'm all right."

"Oh yeah? Then who *is* this Ramón guy?"

She pulled back and frowned.

"I couldn't but help hearing you say his name when you were on the phone."

"Ramón López Oso," she said, "is a sleazebag."

Sleazebag was a funny word to me, but I didn't laugh about it.

After a moment, Barb said, "I'm doing a little job for him."

"Something about Billy?"

Her face went like I'd slapped it. "No," she said. "That's completely different."

Barb was not telling me the truth, but she was a friend now so I said, "I'm not butting into your business. All I want to say is that if I can help you out, I'll try my best."

"I believe you would," she said.

"I would! I would!"

She laughed, and it was a nice sound. I'll put funny bits into my show for sure.

I said, "But what you want most is to meet Billy again, am I right?"

"Do you know where he is?"

"No. But I figure we should go back to the club. I can ask people there if he's coming in tonight. I can say it's because I have to see him. And I do have to see him. In fact, it's urgent."

20.

We didn't get to the Linger Longer till nearly eleven and even then the front door was locked. When I went back to the car to tell Barb, she was disappointed, because she was dressed to kill again. "What do we do now?" she said. "Go home and come back later?"

"Tell you what," I said. "I'll go around the back and see if I can get in. Might be somebody who knows what time Billy's due."

"You want me to come too?"

"You stay in the car. I won't be long."

"O.K.," she said. "These shoes are a bitch anyhow."

I walked around the club to the alley behind it. Ed had said that tonight there was a famous band with a cover charge going to play, so I figured there ought to be someone inside, getting ready for business. And at the back I found some cars parked, but the door I used before was locked. I banged on it, but nobody came.

After that, all I could think of to do was check the windows. I knew which side Billy's office was on, where there was a grass space between the club and the dry cleaners next door. I went that way and took a look in each window as I came to it.

When I saw Billy, I only caught a glimpse, but there wasn't any doubt. He was in his office, all right. But he was in there with Pete!

That shocked and surprised me so much that I stood with my jaw hanging down for as long as a whole moment before I ducked away. And then all I could do was sit underneath the window to try to work it out.

After seeing Pete with Miller, the last place in the world I expected to see Pete was with Billy. I didn't know what he could be there for, but I did know that Billy needed to be told about last night as soon as possible. Maybe it would save him from making a big mistake.

But I sure didn't want to talk to Billy with Pete still there. All I could think of was to stick around and wait for Pete to leave. So I got up and edged towards the back of the club where I could watch the parked cars.

Then I heard a door so I stuck my head around the corner. Just at that very moment Pete ran smack into me.

I said, "Hey! What you think you're doing?"

He grabbed my shirt and he shouted, "I *told* you I saw the little bastard at the window."

Behind Pete Billy walked around the corner. He was smoking a cigar.

Pete said, "What the fuck you up to, runt?"

"Let go of me. Let go!" I twisted and tried to pull away, but all that happened was that my shirt ripped, my *new* shirt. But even it ripping didn't do any good because by then Pete had a two-hand grip on me.

"Billy!" I said. "I saw this guy talking to a cop last night. It was out at the dog place. I came here this morning to warn you.

I think this guy is setting you up. I only came here to help you, Billy. I'm your friend."

And then Pete let me go. I stood there, sweating. I tried to stick the ripped flap of my shirt back onto my chest.

Pete started to laugh. Billy didn't laugh, but he smiled. He said, "You want to tell me about Yount and the cop, huh?"

"That's right! They were talking like big buddies."

"Well," Billy said, "Yount's just been telling me all about there were cops at the Fairgrounds last night."

"*He* told you?"

"And how he spotted you out there too. And then Yount lets out with, 'The little bastard's outside the window!' and runs out of the room. Well, what can I do but tag along to see what's happening?"

I said, "Did he tell you that him and the cop together, they chased me when they saw me?"

"You didn't say you chased him, Yount."

"We didn't."

"Yes they did!" I said.

Pete said, "We shouted at him, and he ran like a weasel. Nobody chased him, but I bet we scared the shit out of him."

Billy gave his head one shake like he was thinking. He said, "And then he shows up outside my window. That's a bit of luck." Billy puffed on his cigar. "But then I always was lucky." And Billy Cigar turned around and headed back to the club.

Pete and I stood there looking after him. There was nothing for us to do but follow.

"You did so chase me," I said.

"Shut the fuck up, runt," he said.

There was no reasoning with the man, so I shut up.

21.

"I'm not a real smart guy," Billy said.

Pete and I had a chair each, but Billy didn't sit down at all. He stood in front of us with his cigar. The way he held it made it look like a gun.

Billy said, "I'm not smart, but I've had some luck. You guys know about Linda and the little job that set us up. Goddamn, if that wasn't shit lucky, because without that, I'd be in jail or something. No cars. No club. No investment portfolio. Nothing. Yessiree, I got lucky. The American dream, that's me. And all I have to do for the rest of my life is protect my god-damn butt. You guys want a drink?"

Pete said, "No."

I didn't want to be like Pete so I said, "I'll have a beer, thanks."

Billy went to the bar. He tossed me a can of beer. He said,

"No, I am not real smart, but one time I heard this thing where a guy said everybody's got a talent for something. You believe that? You think everybody's got a talent?" He looked at Pete and then at me.

I said, "I believe it."

"Well, so do I," Billy said. "And I believe that my talent is for feeling whether things are going to work out. You know what I mean? I had this *feeling* about Linda's idea, and, by Christ, it sure worked out."

"It sure did," I said.

"And now," Billy said, "all of a sudden, I got a situation I'm not smart enough to figure out. I got two guys I never met before a couple of days ago and they both keep showing up and all I ever hear about is some goddamn dogs out at the Fairgrounds. Now, do I care about dogs? Me?" He looked at me and then he looked at Pete.

I said, "Do you?"

Billy said, "No, I do not. I *like* 'em O.K., but I don't *care* about them. But Yount here, he sashays in and he's full of stories about microwaves and fighting pigs and God knows what all. And he doesn't bring his stories to me, he brings them to Linda. And Linda *is* someone who cares about dogs. Now, maybe that's lucky. But maybe, *maybe* it's smart. Is that the way you're smart, Yount? Going to the right person? Because if you'd come to *me* about goddamn microwave hot dogs and dog and hog fights, I'd've sent you packing." He took a puff on his cigar and stared at Pete.

I said, "Thanks a lot for the beer," and pulled the tab.

"And now this guy . . ." Billy turned to me. "This guy at least I understand. He's a little smelly hustler, strictly dime-a-dance, and he's trying to scratch some money off me any old way he can." Billy held up his hand and said to me, "I see you open your mouth, but don't you say nothing."

So I didn't.

"But suddenly this smelly little hustler turns up every day

in a row, and then *he* turns out to have some connection with Yount or the Fairgrounds or the goddamn dogs."

Billy looked back and forth between us. "And then today, today it's cops. You guys tired of talking dogs all of a sudden? I mean, *cops!"*

Billy shook his head. He said, "I'm not a real smart guy. And I'm also not a goddamn Boy Scout. Christ, I've killed guys, you know? I've held guys by the hair and shot their heads off and ruined a silk shirt with the blood. And, the way it goes, can't nobody touch me for it. But I'm going to tell you both something for nothing now. I'll be buttfucked before I let the cops get an angle on me for the sake of some dogs." While Billy took a puff, Pete scratched at his beard.

"But," Billy said, "Linda still wants something done. And Linda is the sort of gal that gets what she wants, you know what I mean? There's a dead guy down South America found that out the hard way. And the ironical thing is, part of the reason he's dead is Linda had some dogs down there and the guy wouldn't let loose of them. Damn, ain't that a laugh?"

Billy looked at each of us before he said, "So if it has four legs and barks Linda sure is the right person. And that makes it tough on me. Linda wants something done at the Fairgrounds, but I don't want to do it. How's a guy that's not so smart supposed to handle that? Huh? Any ideas?"

I didn't have any ideas. Pete didn't say anything either.

Billy said, "No suggestions, fellas? Well, I tell you, I've got me a feeling for how to work this out. You want to hear about my feeling?"

I said, "Sure."

Billy said, "I've got two guys walk in the door, each one of them wants something. Yount says when it's all over he maybe wants a job. And the little guy would crawl on the floor for a nickel. So I'll tell you how this plays, fellas. Here it is. You'll like this."

He looked at Pete as he said, "I want you two guys to take the dog place out for me. You understand? I mean *out.* Am I making myself clear? And I want you to do it together. You work with him. He works with you. Just the two of you. Nobody else. And I want to read about dogs in the newspaper. I want to read about dogs while I'm eating my breakfast. I want indigestion because it's such a sad fucking story. And I want it so there's no hassle to come back to me. You get me? And then I want the two of you to come here and say, 'We done the job like you said, Billy,' and I want for things to be just what you say they are, and nothing more. And if that's how it all happens, I'll look after you guys good. I will. I'll make sure the two of you won't regret it for the rest of your lives. You got my word on that. Scout's honor."

Billy puffed on his cigar. He said, "That's the deal. Now get out of here, the both of you."

There was nothing I wanted more than to get out. I headed for the door, but I did stop, just for a minute, just for Barb. I said, "One thing, Mr. Cigar."

"What the fuck's that?"

"Are you going to be in the club later on tonight?"

22.

I got to the parking lot first, but Pete wasn't more than a couple of seconds behind. "Where are you going?" he called. "Jan! Stop, for Christ's sake!"

I was surprised that he used my real name so I turned around, but I said, "Don't come any closer, you maniac." And he stopped where he was.

"You ripped my best shirt."

"Forget about the shirt," he said.

I started backing away.

"Stop, Jan! We have to talk."

"I don't have to talk," I said. "Are you so stupid you don't understand what Billy wants us to do? You dumb . . . dog-handler! He wants us to *kill* people!"

"Shut up!" Pete said. "Keep your goddamn voice down!"

"I am *not* going to kill anybody! No way! You can't make

me!" Pictures and sounds and feelings were jumping around in my head.

When the policeman who tricked me when I was thirteen led me out of the house, an old woman neighbor waved her finger and said, "Just truly love the Lord and you won't end up like your poppa, hear?"

And at the trial Daddy's lawyer told the prosecutor, "He's got everything his father's got, only less," and they laughed together, and it was about me, and it made me angry and I wanted to kill them both, and the policeman too.

And now I knew what an evil killing bastard Billy Cigar really was. And he was trying to make me do what he'd done and be like him.

And then I remembered Barb, and her waiting for me in her car so she could do some job with Billy Cigar.

"What?"

"Moro?" Suddenly Pete was only a few yards away from me. "Something wrong with you?"

"No!" I said.

"We need to talk."

There was nothing to talk about. I headed for Barb. I got to the grass strip that led to the front of the club when Pete said, "*Please*!"

I was so surprised that he was begging that I did stop. He hadn't moved. He said, as soft as he could, but so's I'd still hear, "Nobody will be killed. I guarantee it."

And that confused me.

"There'll be money in it for you."

That confused me too, because Pete was supposed to be hard-up and looking for a job with Billy Cigar. "How much?" I said.

"We can't sort it out here. Get in my car." He walked over to a beat-up Ford.

I didn't move.

"Come on!" he said. "It'll be serious money. It's a real chance for you. Just get in the goddamn car."

I tried to work it out, but I couldn't. It felt like one of those wrestling things where the bad wrestler offers to shake hands with the good wrestler and you *know* it's a trick, and you shout and shout to him but he won't listen.

Pete got in and sat behind the steering wheel and never took his eyes off me and I just couldn't think of a good reason not to let him say what he had to say, even though I knew how dangerous Pete could be. And then I remembered Billy said Pete and I had to work together. That meant Pete couldn't hurt me. He needed me.

So, I went to his car. But I got in one of the back doors, not the front, and I got in on the passenger side. I figured being that little bit further away from the guy was safer.

Pete said, "Oh, good move, runt," and he started the engine.

"Hey, what're you doing?" I said.

"We can't stay here."

"I don't want to go anyplace else. If you've got something to say, say it." But he just backed the car into the alley.

I realized I'd walked into a trick so I tried to get out, but the door wouldn't open. I tried to roll down the window, but the handle wouldn't turn.

"Central locking," Pete said and his voice was mean, just like he'd been the first time, at the dog place.

He spun his tires on the cinders and then I got thrown against a door when he turned onto the street. Right away he turned the corner in front of the club and I saw we were passing Barb inside her car. I waved and shouted, but she didn't see me.

Then I couldn't think of anything else to do. I sat back and folded my arms across my chest. I still couldn't see any reason for Pete to hurt me.

About ten minutes later Pete pulled into a parking lot behind a flat, brick building. He turned off the engine and leaned over the seat. He said, "I know you must be puzzled about all this. I promise I'll explain it to you soon, but first we got to go in here. I'd appreciate it if you'd just trust me for a couple more minutes and not make a scene."

I didn't say anything and to top it off I kept my arms folded and I looked away.

"Jesus H. Christ," Pete said. "A goddamn attitude now!" He got out and before I knew it, he'd opened a door and grabbed one of my arms. He dragged me clean out of the car, and then he picked me up by the waist. I tried to twist free, but with his other hand he took ahold of my hair. That hurt. I stopped fighting him. Instead I went limp. Dead weight is supposed to be heavier and I hoped he'd get back trouble or something.

Pete carried me on his hip into the building.

I couldn't see much. There were some people standing around and posters on the walls and big potted plants on the floor next to a window.

Pete walked down a hall and then there was a counter with a young guy behind it. A woman was talking to him. Pete hoisted me up and laid me out like a dead squirrel ready for skinning. He took hold of my hair again and leaned on me with an elbow. "Look what the cat drug in," he said.

I was facing the young guy and I saw him back away. He said, "Please, sir, kindly—"

"I'm old and tired and I only got seven toes," Pete said. "I don't have the time or wear left to do this nice. I want to see Carollee, and I want to see her now."

"Who? Who?"

"Hoot Owl, kid. Where the hell is Carollee?"

"I don't think—"

"That's right. Don't think. She in her office?"

"Y . . . yeah."

"Buzz me through then. I know the way."

"I can't do that."

Pete pounded a fist on the desk. "Let me through! Let me through!"

Behind the kid, a door opened. A woman on aluminum crutches came in. "What the hell is all this racket?" she said, and it was the voice of someone in charge.

But I could feel Pete's grip relax. He said, "Hi, honey. Me and my friend were passing by and we thought we'd stop in and say hello."

23.

In the crutch woman's office, Pete said, "Carollee, this is Jan, my good buddy and soon-to-be partner in crime."

I didn't know how he had the nerve to call me his buddy, but I didn't say anything because I was trying to work out where I had seen Carollee before. She looked familiar, dark-haired and with these mixed-color eyes.

She said, "Hello, Jan. I'm pleased to meet you, even if you do keep some bad company." There was a musical sound to her voice, now it was quiet, and that was familiar too. But I couldn't place her. Even so, I could tell right away she wasn't crazy like Pete, though they were some kind of friends. If they hadn't been friends, she'd have called the cops for sure when he made all that ruckus coming in.

I decided to shake her hand. "Hi. Glad to meet you. I'm Jan Moro."

"Jan Moro?" she said. "Are you the man whose friend, Rose Goody, didn't come back from Chicago?"

"How did you know that?"

"You told me about her on the phone yesterday afternoon."

"*You're* Sergeant Fleetwood?"

"I am."

And all of a sudden I remembered where I knew her from. "You've got a TV show about missing kids, right?"

She nodded. "Missing children, missing adults. A cable program."

"I saw your show in a bar a couple of times."

In fact I'd seen it more often than that because the guys in a lot of bars watch it, but they turn it on to look at her, not the missing kids. They say things like, "A cop. What a waste!" Also other stuff that's crude.

"You're a cop!" I said.

"I have that honor and privilege."

Pete laughed when she said that.

I said, "They don't show your crutches on the TV. I didn't realize there were cops with crutches."

"I won't be on them forever," she said.

"Show a little respect," Pete said. "You're in the presence of a certified, Grade-A, shot-on-duty hero."

"Zip it," Sergeant Fleetwood said to him.

"They wanted to give her a medal and put her out to pasture, but she bullied them into letting her prove that she was better on aluminum sticks than most cops are in cleats with a tail wind. But that's only the public heroism. The brass doesn't know about what she goes through, with the operations and the physical therapy—"

"Shut the fuck up!" Sergeant Fleetwood leaned forward and I thought that she was going to jump at him across the desk and do him some damage.

But Pete sure stopped what he was saying. He scratched at his beard and got out of his chair and said, "Look, I've got to make a call to loverboy. Can you look after my diminutive friend for a few minutes?"

"How about you don't come back?" Sergeant Fleetwood was not happy with the guy.

But Pete put a hand on my shoulder and leaned down to my ear. "She loves me really, but she hates to admit it in public."

Sergeant Fleetwood said, "You're not even supposed to be here."

"Do you know how many public phones are out of order?" She didn't say anything to that and Pete and her traded looks, but I guess she was right because he said, "No one said I had to make a religion out of it."

"Do something useful on your way. Ask Eugene to bring us some coffee."

Pete left the room.

When he was gone, Sergeant Fleetwood said, "Sorry for the language a minute ago, but sometimes it's the only way to get the guy to rest his mouth."

"No need to apologize," I said.

"It's not a real polite way to talk," she said.

"To tell you the truth," I said, "it reminded me of my own momma."

"Yeah?"

And it did.

My momma said lots of phrases using the big f word, and when I was little she taught me to say them too because it made her laugh, a little kid using words like that. But then when I started at school what I said made the teachers angry and I didn't know what the problem was and why they were shouting at me. I learned quick enough though, that's one thing I did learn at school. And I don't say any of those big f things now, not myself, though they don't offend me to hear. And I forgive my momma what she did because I know now there weren't many things in her life that made her laugh.

"What?"

"Mr. Moro? Are you all right?"

"Sure. Why?"

"You seemed to have gone someplace else, that's all."

"I was thinking about my momma."

"Oh," Sergeant Fleetwood said. "Does she live in Indianapolis?"

"No. She's long dead."

"I'm sorry."

"Me too."

I think she decided that I didn't want to talk about Momma any more because then she said, "What happened to your shirt?"

"*He* tore it."

"Why?"

"I don't know," I said. "And it was a new shirt too."

"Well, come over here and I'll see if I can do something about it." She opened a drawer in her desk and fished around and pulled out a safety pin.

"That's all right. I'll live," I said.

"Come over here," she said again, and she meant it, so I did. She pinned the torn bit of my shirt in one place and then found two more safety pins and put them in too. Her hands were warm. She said, "Maybe I should keep a sewing basket in the desk."

I thought about saying that depended how often Pete came to see her, but since I didn't know what kind of friends they were, I decided it was better not to say anything than take a chance. I could tell there was part of her that thought he was crazy. That, by itself, was enough to make me like her. She didn't seem like a real cop at all.

She leaned back and took a look. "There, you're decent again."

"Thanks," I said.

"I haven't had much luck finding your friend Rose yet. Have you checked her house? It'd be nice to think she's made it back home by herself."

"I went there last night after I talked to you, but I haven't been up today."

"Maybe you can do that later."

"I will if I can," I said.

"I asked Missing Persons in Chicago to send someone to the sister's house. All I can do now is wait for them to fax me a report on what they find out."

Then there was a knock on the door and a young man carried a tray in. He looked so pale and wispy he must have spent his whole life indoors. I found a set of exercise weights in a box in an alley once. If I hadn't already sold them, they would've done this kid some good.

He said, "I didn't know what your guest wanted in his coffee, Carollee, so I brought the half-and-half and the brown sugar."

"That's fine, Eugene."

"You're welcome," and he left.

"Mr. Moro, why don't you add the cream and sugar for yourself so it's how you like it."

"O.K. Can I do yours?"

"I drink mine black," she said, so I passed her one of the cups as it was.

For me it's lots of cream and four spoons of sugar, when I can get it. "Good coffee," I said.

"Is Rose a close friend, if you don't mind my asking? It's just that you seemed so upset when we talked yesterday."

"Yeah, a close friend," I said.

"I was surprised when Homer called me. He's never asked for this kind of favor before, so he must be pretty worried about Rose too."

It sounded like she wanted me to say something nice about Sergeant Proffitt, and I was working out what it could be when Pete came back into the room. Right away he said to me, "Who's been a naughty boy?"

"What?"

"No coffee for me?" He went out again.

I'd been feeling so comfortable that I'd just about completely forgotten Pete. I wondered if I should have taken the chance to get away while he was making his phone call.

On the other hand, if I'd of run for it, then maybe Sergeant Fleetwood would stop trying to find Rosie, even though it was Proffitt that got her started with that and not Pete. And there was still what Pete had said about money. Everything was sure confusing and it was hard to know the best thing to do.

And then I remembered Sergeant Fleetwood's TV show. If I could talk to her about it right, maybe she'd help me set mine up. That brought me back to thinking about Billy. If there *was* a way for me and Pete to do what Billy wanted without killing somebody, then maybe I could still get him to sponsor me. I'd take his money even though I didn't like him anymore. When you're in business, you can't afford to be too fussy. I bet lots of people with TV shows don't like their sponsors.

"What?"

"Mr. Moro? You were away again."

"I bet you didn't know I've got plans for a TV show myself," I said.

But before she could say anything to that, Pete came back carrying a cup. "Yes, a naughty, naughty boy," he said. He moved a chair next to mine and sat down. "You were supposed to call Carollee's pal, Homer Proffitt, this morning."

What with one thing and another calling Proffitt had entirely escaped out of my head. But I said, "How'd *you* know that?"

"Homer Proffitt is not happy with you, Jan Moro. He counted on hearing your dulcet tones while he made breakfast for whoever he shared his bed with last night. You have dog-dooed on all his best laid plans, but don't rush to the phone now to make amends. I've offered your profuse and humble apologies."

Pete had just been on the phone with Proffitt. Last night I'd seen him talking to Miller. "You're a cop!" I said.

Pete stuck out a hand. "Lieutenant Leroy Powder. Pleased to meet you, Mr. Starch."

24.

I could hardly believe it. I knew Pete was evil enough to be a cop. But when I thought about how he threatened me at the dog place, and what he told Billy and Linda about Cobb microwaving the puppy, and that he was at the Linger Longer warning Billy today . . . "But if you're a cop," I said, "then—"

"Then things are not what they seem. And you, Clarence Starch, Junior, are in shit up to your earlobes."

"But—"

"Homer Proffitt has set up a meeting. That's where we'll sort out what's going to happen to you."

"But I haven't done anything!"

Sergeant Fleetwood said, "You owe Mr. Moro an explanation, Roy."

"Oh do I?" Pete said. "Has Mr. Moro got so many ants in his britches that he can't wait till three-thirty?"

I didn't know what he meant about a meeting and my britches. All I knew was that Pete was a cop! Cops have done the worst things that ever happened in my life. I didn't want an explanation. I didn't want anything at all. I stood up. "You can keep your money. I don't want it."

Pete grabbed for my arm, but I shook him off. Even so he said, "Sit down."

"I don't want to sit down! I haven't done anything! You can't make me sit down!"

Pete said, "Put your butt on that chair or you'll be locked up quicker than you can blink."

"I haven't done anything!"

"Sit *down*!"

I sat down. I said, "What's this meeting? Who's it with? What's it got to do with me?"

"Loverboy Proffitt has invited every important player in Operation Judgment Day."

"In what?"

"Jan, old buddy, I'm just an ignorant hired hand myself. I tell you, we're both rudderless submarines in an IPD cesspit and even I don't know exactly who or what all the other sailors are."

Sergeant Fleetwood said, "But the difference between your position and Mr. Moro's is that poor Mr. Moro is caught up in this through no fault of his own."

"The veracity of that hypothesis is one of the things to be assessed later today."

"What's that supposed to mean?" she said.

"Your affectionate friend Homer agrees with you that Jan-Clarence Moro-Starch got involved by accident, but more important people aren't so sure. They think he may be working undercover himself."

They both looked at me. There seemed to be a pause so I said, "Before this meeting can we go to 24th Street? I want to see if Rosie is back."

I sat in the front seat next to Pete this time. I didn't want to be there, of course, but one of my philosophies is to row with the current when the river's rising and when he threatened to lock me up, I believed him. But I didn't feel much like talking.

Pete didn't say anything for a long time himself, but then he said, "Who the hell is this Rosie?" But I didn't like the way he asked, so I didn't answer.

When we got close he said, "Which house is it?"

"Two in from the corner. The one that used to be green. Where that wagon is."

Pete parked behind the station wagon.

"Hey," I said. "The front door's open."

"So your friend's back after all."

"No! Rosie would never leave the door open, not in this neighborhood."

Pete looked at the front of the house and then back to me. "Are you sure?"

"I'm sure!" And I was. She wouldn't.

"I suppose you want to go in and check it out." He fiddled with his belt. "I'm getting old," he said. "I forgot to pat you down. You don't have a gun on you, by any chance?"

"A gun? No." I didn't think he meant the gun I have buried downtown.

He hit the dashboard with a fist. "There's no radio in this crate," he said. He looked at me. "So what do you think, runt? Do we go in naked, or do we find a phone and call for help?"

"Rosie would *hate* a stranger messing with her things. I'm going in," I said, "but you can wait out here if you want to."

I tried the door handle. This one, the front seat, worked. As I got out, Pete did too. I could hear noises from inside the house and they were rough, banging sounds. Pete said, "Oh well, plenty of people think I've lived too long already."

25.

When we got to the porch, I showed Pete which planks were safe to step on. Up close we could see splintered wood and that the door had been pried open.

We went inside and I could tell that the banging sounds were coming from the kitchen, which was at the back of the house, but before we got there a guy walked right past the open doorway carrying a drawer. He didn't see us. We heard him empty the drawer and we heard him say, "What a load of fucking crap!"

Pete mouthed, "On three." Then he held up one finger, two fingers, three.

We rushed into the kitchen and before the guy knew what hit him, Pete spread him out and pushed his face down on Rosie's kitchen table. That must have hurt because the table was where he'd been emptying the drawers.

"All right, motherfucker," Pete said, "you got five seconds to tell us what you're doing in here."

The guy made sounds, but he didn't make sense.

I said to Pete, "Lift him up a little. I think his mouth's on a roll of paper towels."

"This is no time to play good mugger, bad mugger," Pete said, but he eased off.

The guy's face came up saying, "Don't hurt me! Don't hurt me! I'll give you my wallet. I've got a wife. I've got four little kids."

Pete said to me, "I'll take the wallet. You take the wife and kids." He let the guy stand and said, "Where's the wallet?" The guy began to reach inside his coat, but Pete pushed him down on the table again. "I asked where it was, I didn't say to get it out."

"Inside pocket."

When the guy was standing again, Pete pulled the wallet out and went through it. "Hundred and sixty-seven bucks," he said, and for a minute I thought he was going to take it, but he looked at the documents instead. "All right, Nick, what are you doing here?"

"I've got a right."

"No you haven't!" I said.

"You don't live here," Pete said. "You live on East 54th Street."

"This is my mother's house."

"Rose Goody's your mother?" Pete said.

"Yeah."

I said, "Where is she? Where is she?"

"Chicago. She had a heart attack two days ago. Keeled over in her sister's living room."

"Is she all right?" I asked.

"She won't last long."

The guy said it without the littlest feeling, and I remembered how Rosie had said her son thought she wasn't good enough to be his mother.

Pete said, "So where is she, Nick? In a hospital?"

"Yeah."

"She won't like that," I said.

The guy saw me for the first time. "You know her?"

"Yeah I know her."

"You know if she's got any insurance? Because her fucking sister's trying to unload her on me and I'll be damned if she's going to croak on my bank account."

I made a move at the guy when he said that. If the table hadn't been between us, I would have slugged him.

He jumped back.

Pete said, "Nicholas Goody, is that Rosie's son's name?"

"Yeah," I said.

Pete gave the wallet back and Goody counted the money before he put it away.

Pete said to me, "Do you know where insurance policies and other personal documents might be?"

They were under Rosie's stairs, in a special box I'd built for her near the bottom. He'd never find them. "No," I said.

"Sorry we can't help, Nick," Pete said.

I said, "There was no reason to make all this mess. Rosie hates mess."

"She'll never be back here," he said.

"But I will be," I said. "And if it isn't cleaned up the way you found it, and the door fixed, I'll come to East 54th and splatter your face on your own kitchen table, personally. That's a promise."

He stiffened a little. He said, "I was going to straighten up anyway."

"Come on," I said to Pete, "before I do something I'd regret."

When we got into the car, Pete said, "You're a feisty little devil when you're roused."

"He shouldn't be in Rosie's house."

Pete said, "Do you have anything to write with? Pen, pencil?"

"Why?"

"I want to run a check on Nick's plate number."

"Sorry," I said.

He read the license plate out loud, then said, "Time was I could have remembered it."

"I'll remember," I said. I put my hands over my eyes and repeated it back to him.

He started the car. "Hate makes the memory stronger, huh?" We drove away.

I didn't watch which way we went. I didn't care much. I was thinking about Rosie.

But Pete said, "You want to know something? Make you a better . . . Make you understand people better?"

"What?"

"We burst in on that guy's life like a fucking thunderstorm, right?"

"Yeah."

"Well, when Nick Goody tells the story, he's going to say we had guns. Both of us. He's even going to remember it that way, because he was so scared. Tells you something about witnesses, doesn't it, because I promise, that's the way he'll tell it to his friends."

"No he won't," I said.

"What do you know about it?"

"A guy like that won't have any friends."

Pete laughed hard and nearly ran into the back of a car in front of us.

I didn't see why it was funny, but I didn't say anything and just thought about how Rosie would hate strangers going through her things, and for sure her son was a stranger.

26.

After a while Pete said, "I've got two calls to make. I want to check on Goody's car, and I want to tell Carollee about Rosie's heart attack. She can find out which hospital Rosie's in and maybe even what the doctors have to say."

I saw that we were stopped in front of a public phone in a shopping center. The phone was on the wall between a drug store and a laundromat.

Pete said, "Runt, it's important that you don't try to run away or anything."

"What? Oh. No, I won't run away."

"I've decided that Carollee's right."

"What about?"

"Proffitt and Miller have taken advantage of you."

"They have?"

"But if you play it right, you can come out of this pretty well."

I didn't understand what he was saying, but I said, "How?" Sometimes if you let a body keep talking you can catch up with what they're meaning by the end.

"Look," Pete said, "I've only been in Operation Judgment Day a few weeks and all they brought me in for was to set up the dogs at the Fairgrounds."

"You set that up?"

"It's a long story," Pete said. "But the point is that the department let me spend whatever I wanted. I can't believe they financed it just by cutting crime prevention programs, so they must have a Federal grant or something. But I do know that Operation Judgment Day started a long time before I got involved and from what I can make out they haven't once not done something because it cost too much. So I can't see why they shouldn't offer you real money to help them get what they want."

"What do they want?"

"Billy Sigra," he said.

"This whole thing is about the cops getting Billy?"

"Yup."

"I didn't know he was that important," I said.

"Runt, my friend, you've hit the intergalactic ray gun on its firing button there. Why *is* the man worth all this fuss?"

"Why?"

"I don't know," he said.

"But you're working with them."

"I'm working *for* them. There's a difference."

"I don't get it," I said.

"I know I've jerked you around," Pete said, "but that's just the way I am. From here on in, though, I'll do the best I can to get you a whole heap of cash."

Pete had said a lot of things that were new to me, but the newest of all was that here he was talking to me like I was a human person. And to tell the truth, it made me uncomfortable.

It's not that I didn't like it better that way, but it was so hard to believe I could trust him.

"Runt?"

"What?"

"Did you hear me?"

"Tell me something," I said.

"What's that?"

"You like Sergeant Fleetwood, don't you?"

I guess he wasn't expecting the question, though it seemed logical enough to me. He squinted up his face and I thought maybe he was going to become the old Pete again. But then he said, "Yeah, you could say that."

"Does she like you?"

He thought about that before he said, "She used to. But, it's just not as simple as it was."

"Because of Proffitt?"

He laughed. "Homer fucking Proffitt. I cannot *bear* that phony Southern charm and it purely defeats me to understand how a woman with half a brain can go for it. The guy would sell his granny to get a good arrest, but Carollee's by no means the only one who either doesn't see it or doesn't care. Still, she's a big girl, even if she does live in dreamland about running a marathon one of these days." He scratched at his beard. "So why the questions?"

"I don't trust you," I said. "But I trust her."

He laughed again, louder. "You're a helluva fucking guy, runt. You really are. Tell you what. Call her yourself and check out whether you can trust me."

So I did. I remembered the number, and I had him sit in the car. I even said, "Don't you run away or anything."

"Mr. Moro?" Sergeant Fleetwood said. "Did you find Rose at home?"

"No," I said. "She's in the hospital in Chicago with a heart attack."

"Oh no!"

"*He'll* tell you about it in a minute. But there's something else."

"What's that?"

"He's been talking all kinds of stuff to me, telling me what I ought to do. Now excuse me for saying it, because I know he's a friend of yours, but if I do what he wants me to do, am I going to get screwed? Pardon the language, but even when he's being nice there's something about the guy that scares me and part of me thinks I ought to light out next chance I get, even though I haven't done anything."

"Roy will deal straight with you," she said.

"You say that even though you don't like him so much anymore?"

"Even though *what*?"

"I asked him whether he liked you and whether you liked him, that's all."

"And what did he say?"

"That he liked you, all right, but with you it wasn't as simple as it used to be."

"You asked Leroy Powder . . ." And now it was her laughing and it was so loud that I had to take the phone away from my ear.

"What's so funny?" I said when she calmed down.

"Is he there? Can you put him on? Unless there's something else you want to ask me?"

"I'll get him, but he doesn't have a pencil," I said. "So maybe you could write down this license plate number." And I told her Nicholas Goody's number.

"O.K., I've got that," she said.

"And do you think you could find out which hospital in Chicago Rosie's at?"

"O.K."

"And whether the doctors say she's going to be all right and when they'll let her out."

"I'll find out everything I can, Mr. Moro," she said.

"Thanks," I said, and then I called Pete over, and said that I would wait for him in the laundromat.

Laundromats are good. They're always warm from the dryers and nobody gives you a hard time for waiting around, especially if you sit in front of a machine that's got clothes in it. I like dryers best, because there's more to watch.

In this place, there was only one dryer with clothes in it, so that's where I sat down. The clothes dropping across the glass were mostly white, but there were a few things with patterns in purple and yellow and green. Each rotation was a little bit different.

I sat thinking for a long time. When I started talking to Sergeant Fleetwood I was worrying about who to trust, but when I asked her to find out about Rosie it hit me for the first time that Rosie might die.

That's not what I wanted to happen. And I realized that what I wanted more than anything was to go to Chicago to see Rosie, to see how she was for myself, and that as soon as Sergeant Fleetwood found out which hospital she was in then I could just take off. I wanted to tell Rosie I knew how much she must be hating to be in a strange hospital. I wanted to tell her that I would help her to come back to her own home. I could shop and cook for her and look after her till she was stronger and I could sleep out back because I knew she never wanted me to move in with her permanent. There were two walls of a garage behind her house and I could fix them up to be real cozy, no problem.

And I got to thinking about all the house improvements I could make, and I got to thinking about old times.

After a while a woman opened the dryer even though the machine hadn't stopped. The clothes must have been dry enough, though, because she started taking them out. And then she turned around and put her hands on her hips. It was only then I noticed that Pete was sitting next to me. The woman said, "What are you two looking at?"

"What?" I said.

"You get your kicks from women's underwear? Is that it? Because I'm going to call the cops. That's what I'm going to do, I'm going to call the cops!"

"Come on," Pete said to me.

"What?" I said.

"Yeah," the woman said. "You fuck off! Both of you!"

Pete took my elbow and led me out and back to the car.

I was sad and tired and fed up and slow and lost and alone and especially confused from everything that was happening to me.

Pete put me in the car and then got in himself. He said, "Number one, unfortunately, Goody's clean. Number two, unfortunately, you got a big mouth. You know that?" But maybe he saw that I didn't feel so good because he said, "Carollee says to say how sorry she is about Rosie." He started the car up and we drove for a while. He said, "Carollee also says that I gotta take care of our little Cupid. Feed you. Shit like that. You hungry?"

I didn't say anything.

"Well, I am," he said. "And I know just the place."

27.

The place was a restaurant and it was way on the edge of town and in an enormous mall, except that it stood by itself in the parking lot. Just inside the door we got stopped by a woman standing next to a cash register. She said, "How can we serve you boys today?"

"What do you want, runt?" Pete said.

"What?"

"Haven't you ever been to a Guzzler before?"

"I don't know what you're talking about."

"My kid loves it here."

"You have a kid?"

"Give him a full rack of ribs," Pete said. "Myself, I'll have the broiled halibut."

He gave the woman some money. She made change and then she said, "This is Stephanie, your hostess for today. She will take you to the ingestion area of your choice." And suddenly there was this other woman, who was smiling like a banana, and she said, "Smoking or nonsmoking?"

"Nonsmoking," Pete said.

"By a window or interior location?"

"Window."

"Light classical or soft rock?"

"Soft rock," Pete said.

"Picnic table or American colonial?"

"I like the idea of picnic," Pete said, "but chairs are so much more comfortable, don't you think?"

"Right this way, fellas," Stephanie said.

Pete pushed me to follow her. On the way we passed by a kind of island with people circling around it and stacking salads and cold stuff on plates. And then we passed another island, with hot vegetables, bacon and sausage gravy.

I should have been in heaven. But I wasn't. I was thinking about poor Rosie, trapped in a strange bed.

When we got sat down, Pete stood up again. "Runt, you coming?"

"Where?"

"While we wait for the meat, we go to the hot and cold bars. You can have as much of anything as you want."

"I'm not real hungry."

"Yeah, all right, stay here. I'll bring you some."

Thinking about Rosie and Pete talking about food reminded me Rosie told me a story once that happened to a friend of hers. The friend had a husband who got drunk every Friday night. He didn't hit her or anything, but he always had to be carried home and it was usually by the same guys he drank with each week.

Well, Rosie's friend got so she'd go out herself on a Friday night—just to see her mother—and she'd come back late enough that her husband would already be asleep on the couch where the guys that brought him home would leave him.

Well, this one time there was a new guy at the bar where the husband drank and the new guy was a joker. He helped carry the husband home but when they were in the house, this new guy figured he deserved a beer for all his effort so he went to the refrigerator. Well, there was no beer, but he noticed that Rosie's friend had some hot dogs in there. So the new guy took a hot dog out and he went to the husband, and undid the fly on the husband's pants. What he did was put the hot dog hanging out like it was the husband's tallywhacker.

Well, Rosie's friend came home and walked in the door and saw her husband on the couch. And she near enough had a heart attack.

"What's the big deal?" Rosie said she asked her friend. "Ain't nothing you ain't seen before."

"The big deal," the friend said, "was that our goddamn cat was sitting on my old man's lap and it had near enough eaten the thing half in two."

"What?"

"I said, 'Runt, are you laughing or eating?' "

Then I saw there was a huge plate of ribs sitting in front of me. Next to that was a plate of vegetables and salads.

"Got to eat if you're ever going to grow up," Pete said. He pointed to a pitcher. "Sauce." He pointed to the food islands. "As much as you want. Dig in."

I was going to say again that I wasn't hungry, but remembering Rosie's story made her feel more alive to me, and that made me feel more alive too. I began to pick at one of the ribs. It wasn't bad. I had some more.

I like it when people tell me stories. Sometimes it seems that's about all there is.

I said to Pete, "I didn't know you had a kid. Is that a boy or a girl?"

"Boy," he said without looking up. He took a big bite of his fish. "Kid lives off dead animals. That's why I'm sitting here with you today."

"How's that?" I said.

"Couple years ago the kid was looking for a life. I gave him some land and some money I had and he built a pet crematorium. Only it didn't work out. There's a whole lot more to the dead pet business than Ricky—that's the kid—and Peggy—that's his wife— realized."

"It's sure not easy being in business," I said.

"But then they got a contract for picking up dead animals off the roads. You know, the animals that get hit by cars."

"Uh-huh."

"So now they use the crematorium for that, a whole new business risen out of the ashes, so to speak, and Ricky says they're good at it. You got any idea what constitutes being good at burning dead animals scraped off the roadside? I don't, but somebody somewhere said something to somebody and now they've got two more contracts and business is booming."

"You must be proud," I said.

Pete picked at his beard. "Yeah."

"But how does that—"

"I'm getting to it," he said. "Once I set the kid up, I decided to go back on active duty, and I wangled myself into a special unit even though they already had a lieutenant. Hey, she'd like you, Turk would. She's got this thing about short men."

"Uh, I don't think—"

"So I made my big comeback and mostly what I do now for IPD is guard VIPs who come to town. Well, a year ago August I drew this guy from Finland and he wanted to see the State Fair. While I was guarding him in the Pig Hall, I overheard three guys talking about dog and hog fights, which was the first I'd ever heard of such a thing. Did you ever hear of that?"

"Not before I was there when you told Billy and Linda."

"Well, I'd heard turf 'n' surf but never of dog 'n' hog. I decided to check it out. I tried to get official backing, but I ended up worrying at the thing in all my spare time. And then I wrote a report. The report lays it out how if IPD and the state work together, they could kill this dog 'n' hog thing dead in Indiana.

They could probably track it down through the whole country. You'd be amazed what a big deal it is. They've even got guys who cross pigs with wild boars so their fighting hogs will have tusks."

"I remember. You said."

"I laid it out good in my report, everything in short words and simple sentences."

"And?"

"And nothing. They said it was too hard for them to work with other state agencies. So I said I'd set the whole thing up for them but then they said they didn't have the money. And that pissed me off, because anything they really want to do they can find money for. They *say* they're still studying the feasibility but that's to keep me from going to the papers, which I still might do even though I'd get kicked off the force. Those ribs all right?"

"Yeah, they're good," I said.

"But then, out of the blue, three and a half weeks ago Homer fucking Proffitt called me. Carollee'd told him about my dog and hog report. And Homer fucking Proffitt said he was part of something called Operation Judgment Day that wasn't going very well and they thought my 'expertise' on dog and hog fighting was exactly what they needed."

Pete stopped to eat a few mouthfuls, but I could tell he had more of the story in mind and was just having a rest to think it out.

After a while he said, "Suddenly, Leroy Powder was in demand again. And suddenly everything had to be done right away. So, for the last three weeks I've been putting together the damn fine hog-fighting dog–training facility that you walked into last Wednesday. And that's how we come to be sitting here today, runt, because I gave my retirement land and nest egg to my kid so him and his missus could burn dead animals. And do you know what I hate most about this whole thing? What I hate the *most*? It isn't that IPD won't do something that ought to be done. It isn't even that they make use of my own-time work without so much as a thank-you. You know what I hate most?"

"What?"

"That as recently as three and a half weeks ago Homer fucking Proffitt was talking to Carollee. She said they broke up last spring. Hey, do you want some dessert?"

28.

When we left the restaurant, Pete said we weren't but ten minutes from the place of the big meeting so we got into his car. Only instead of starting it up he turned my way and said, "Do you know why someone becomes a cop?"

I was surprised by the question, and I sure didn't know the answer.

"Because being a cop, being a good cop, that's a way you can help people."

"It is?"

"And today," Pete said, "today I am going to help you."

"Me?"

"But before I do, I need to make something window-glass clear."

"What?"

"Billy Sigra is vicious. He's an unremorseful killer. He's brutal and vulgar and he's not a real nice guy. Am I right?"

I didn't know what he was getting at. Still, I said, "Yeah."

"But runt, get this into your pint-sized brain: if you let me down, if you cross me up, if you say one thing and do another, if you sell me out, you will wish you were locked for the rest of your life in a six-foot room with Billy fucking Sigra instead of what I will do to you myself."

Pete was the mean Pete from the dog place all over again.

He started the car.

Pete never said where we were going but when we passed a park I know I could tell it was towards Broad Ripple, which is a part of town I go to when I've got something arty to sell. It's way up on the north side and it has rich stores.

Thinking of Broad Ripple reminded me of a story I heard in a bar one time, about this guy who bought a Porsche for fifty bucks.

The guy was looking for a car and he saw this ad in the paper, "Two-year-old Porsche, excellent condition, $50." He thought it was a printing mistake, but what the hell and he called the number and a woman answered and she said, "No, it's not a mistake, but I need to sell the car right away."

Well, the guy knew something had to be wrong, but he decided to go out to the house anyway, and it was a very rich place. And, sure enough, in the driveway there was this Porsche parked and it was blood red and it had nineteen thousand miles on the clock and not a scratch.

So the guy went to the door and a rich-looking woman answered and she offered him a drink and before long they'd done their business. Yes, that was the car. Yes, the asking price was fifty dollars.

Well, one tire was more than worth the fifty bucks so the guy didn't need to look under the hood. He gave the woman the money and didn't even haggle and they did the paperwork and she gave him the keys.

Then, just before he left, he asked her. "I've got to know," he said. "That car. It's worth a small fortune, so why have you just sold it to me for fifty dollars?"

And the woman said, "Last week my husband ran off to Florida with a nineteen-year-old. Two days ago he sent me a telegram. It said, 'Keep the house, but sell the Porsche for whatever you can get and send me the money.' If I put the fifty bucks in an envelope, would you mind mailing it for me?"

"What?"

"Runt, are you putting down roots?"

When I got out and looked I could tell where we were, across the canal from the main part of Broad Ripple and parked outside a store that was closed. There was old furniture in the window, but the window was dirty and a bureau was halfway blocking the front door.

Pete led me around the side. Near the back suddenly Miller came out of a door. He said, "Two of them will be late but we can start without them."

"Party time," Pete said to me.

But Miller said, "Not him."

"What do you mean 'not him'?" Pete said.

"He waits outside."

"Like hell he does," Pete said. "Come on, runt." He pushed in past Miller. I didn't know what to do, but I heard Pete say, "Either he comes in or I leave."

Then from further inside I heard another voice and it said, "Is there a problem, Jerry?"

Miller was still in the doorway and he turned and pointed a finger at me. He said, "Don't move," and he went inside after Pete.

But it wasn't long before Pete came back and said, "Step this way, sir. We've decided to overlook the fact you're not wearing a tuxedo."

"What's that mean?"

"Are you coming in or not?"

Pete'd already warned me what would happen if I crossed him, so I went in.

There was a short hallway to a room and Miller was already about to the door. Pete followed him and I followed Pete and when we got inside it was just a room with a table and seven chairs. There were two guys already in it. One was sitting and it was Sergeant Proffitt. The other was standing and he was skinny and had eyes that bugged out and I'd never seen him before.

Miller said, "Fred, this is Lieutenant Leroy Powder."

Fred was also bald as a coot bird, about forty years old and a fidgeter. He shook hands with Pete in a jerky little way, but his voice was deep and a strong one. He said, "Fred Feske. Pleased to meet you at last, Lieutenant. You're making a fine contribution to Operation Judgment Day."

Then Miller and Fred turned to me. Miller said, "And this is the infamous Clarence Starch, Junior."

"Mr. Starch, Fred Feske." And Fred stuck out his hand.

I shook with him but I made a point of saying, "Jan Moro. Pleased to meet you."

"Sit down," Miller said.

I went for a chair that faced a window. It opened out onto some trees, and I could see the canal from it.

And then I remembered there was this guy at the home in Lafayette and he took kids out fishing sometimes. Once me and two other new kids went out with him and it was a rowboat on a lake and we had to put worms on hooks and one of the other kids didn't like that.

But it didn't bother me, so I even baited the squeamish kid's hook for him, and the others all caught something—sunfish or perch—but I didn't catch a thing.

Then I got a bite and that was exciting because it fought hard and felt heavy and for a minute I thought maybe mine was going to be the biggest fish of the day, only when I pulled it in, what came out of the water wasn't a fish at all, but a turtle. I can still remember the outline of his little body and his four little legs against the sky.

The fishing guy said, "Snapper," meaning a snapping turtle. He took my line and grabbed the turtle by its shell. "The best thing for a snapper," he said, "is a dull knife."

Then he took a knife and cut the turtle's head right off and he wanted me to take my hook out only I wouldn't touch the turtle's head and he got mad and looked at me about the same way he had looked at the turtle and I got scared.

"What?" I felt a hand about on my neck. I nearly jumped out of my skin.

Pete was shaking me, and then I saw Fred was standing near a little Frigidaire with the door open. "You've been asked if you want something to drink, runt. For Christ's sake, you got no manners?"

"I'll have a beer," I said.

"Nothing alcoholic, I'm afraid," Fred said. "Mineral water. Hawaiian Punch. V8. Dr Pepper."

"Any Kool-Aid?"

"Give him water," Miller said.

Fred pulled out a little bottle of water and then he put it on the table in front of me.

"Right," Miller said, "before the others get here I think we can sort out item one, don't you?"

"I think so," Fred said and he turned to me.

Miller said, "We want to know who you work for, Starch."

"Me?"

"You."

"I'm self-employed."

Miller said, "Who do you *work* for?" And then he started talking about how it couldn't be an accident that I showed up at the Fairgrounds at the exact important time for what they were doing and that then I went straight to Proffitt and brought up the subject of Billy Cigar.

Miller kept talking on and on but the longer he talked the less attention I paid. I wanted to be someplace else. It's always been like that with me, right from when I went to school. At school they were forever trying to teach me stuff when I didn't want to learn it, so I stopped going.

"Starch?"

They were all looking at me.

The room was quiet and nobody said anything, so I said, "Water'll be just fine," and I took the little bottle in front of me and twisted off the top.

Miller said, "Nothing to say for yourself?"

Since I hadn't paid him no mind, I didn't know what he wanted me to talk about but I said, "For a start, you and Proffitt still owe me money for last night."

Miller didn't answer that. In fact, nobody said anything at all and they looked around at each other and what I really wanted to do was leave. I said, "I'm a businessman, so I've got a deal for you."

Fred sat up like he'd had a string pulled.

Miller said, "What fucking deal?"

"I've tried to help you guys out, right? But it seems like I keep getting in your way instead so the deal is, if you send me to Chicago, I'll stay up there till you say it's O.K. for me to come back to Indy."

Miller looked at Fred and then at Proffitt and then Pete and still nobody said anything. I tried to think of a simpler way to put it. I said, "If you don't have time to get the Chicago ticket yourself, just give me money and I'll leave you guys to get on with your own business, which I'm sure is real important."

But at first nobody said anything to that either and I was running out of ideas.

Then Pete said, "I've spent the last four hours with Mr. Moro and I believe him to be exactly what he says he is and that his involvement in all this is purely accidental."

"For what it's worth," Proffitt said, "I think the guy's straight too."

Miller said to Pete, "This is a vital decision, Powder."

"It's my butt on the chair," Pete said. "And don't forget, Sigra specifically wants me and Moro to handle Cobb together."

"That's no problem," Fred said, "Cobb can kill Moro before you kill him."

Miller said, "It would be easy to go that way."

Fred said, "And it keeps us from relying on someone nobody knows."

Pete shook his head and said, "Sigra wants me and Moro to kill Cobb together. He'll trust me more if we do it exactly how he wants it done."

I couldn't believe it! After all his soft soap, suddenly Pete was talking about killing people again!

I jumped up. "No way am I going to kill *anybody*! My daddy didn't even do it on purpose, though where he is he's got to act like he did so's they don't pick on him."

Miller said, "What's your problem, Starch?"

"You can't make me kill anybody! You can't make me!"

Fred said, "I think he's showing us what a risk he is right now."

Pete said, "He just doesn't understand what's going on."

While they were talking to themselves I began to walk around the chairs towards the way out.

Pete said, "Sit down, runt."

"I'm not going to kill anybody!"

"Sit *down*!"

I sat down.

Pete scratched at his beard. Then he said, "While we're on the subject of not understanding, I don't know what's going on here either."

"What's that supposed to mean?" Miller said.

"It means it'd be a good time for someone to explain this whole thing to *me*."

Fred said, "Why don't we all calm down and address items one at a time."

What Fred addressed first was a glass and he poured some Dr Pepper into it.

Miller said, "I think Fred's suggestion is a good one."

But Pete was not calming down. He said, "Who the fuck *is*

'Fred,' Captain? What's his status around here? Who does he work for? Because I've never met the guy until today, but the longer we sit here, the more he acts like it's him in charge and not you. Sir."

Miller did not like the trouble Pete was causing. He said, "I am in charge, Powder. And you'd do well to remember that."

"The question stands. Who is Fred Feske? Is he Fred the Fed, or what?"

"You get told what you need to know," Miller said. "We have more important things to do than satisfy your curiosity."

"I'd've thought my curiosity was pretty important," Pete said, "what with it being my butt on the chair with Billy Sigra."

"I'm warning you, Powder," Miller said, but he never told what he was warning Pete about. They just stood glaring at each other.

Proffitt interrupted them not speaking to say, "Captain, maybe y'all could talk more freely if I take Mr. Moro someplace else."

That sounded good to me but Pete said, "No. Moro's butt's in the same chair as mine. He's entitled to hear who he's dealing with too."

Miller banged a fist on the table, so hard that all the bottles and cans fell over. But he didn't care. He just said, "I know all about you, Powder," and his voice was twice as quiet as it was before, but it felt twice as loud. "I was against involving you from the start. If there's a hard way to do something, that's the way you do it. If you can make trouble, you make it. That's the message written all over your record. You've been like that ever since you put on the badge."

"I believe a cop should do things the right way and treat people with some respect," Pete said. "If you're not up to that, tough. If you want me to leave now, fine."

Then Fred said, "Gentlemen, please!" which made them both look his way, so he said, "Lieutenant Powder, I used to be with the Justice Department, but now I am the Chief Security Consultant for Loftus Pharmaceuticals."

Miller sat down. Pete turned slowly towards Fred.

Fred said, "William Sigra's notoriety as a mass murderer covers almost all of Spanish-speaking South America. The fact that he still leads a free and easy life in Indianapolis keeps interfering with the Loftus development program down there. So I approached the Indianapolis Police Department on Loftus's behalf to see if we could help the police create an operation designed to bring Sigra to justice."

Pete stared at the guy. "Let me get this right. You're not a cop of any kind?"

"Not anymore."

"Not state? Not federal?"

"No."

"And you work for a drug company?"

"We prefer the word 'pharmaceutical.' "

Then we all heard someone banging on the outside door.

29.

Miller said, "Take a break," and he left the room.

Proffitt started to mop up the wet mess on the table.

Pete sat down, but he never took his eyes off Fred.

When Miller came back he wasn't alone. The person following him was Cobb!

I'd've run, if I wasn't sitting down, but then I saw that this Cobb was different from the wicked Cobb I met out at the dog place. This Cobb smiled and he said, "Hi guys," and they all said, "Hi," back.

Then Miller said, "Sergeant Terzick, this is Fred Feske," and while the two of them shook hands I just about realized that Cobb was a cop too.

Miller said, "And I believe you've already met the little guy."

Cobb came over to my chair and between him being so big and me being sat down I got scared again even though he was smiling and had his hand out.

But then the smile went and suddenly Cobb looked as mean as hell, and he said, "Oh yeah, I know Jan Moro all right. Just the right size for my microwave oven." And he growled at me! He really growled!

I didn't know where to turn or what to do but then Cobb laughed again and stepped back and he said to Miller, "God, I love doing the *evil* thing. When I heard that Powder told Sigra's missus that I microwaved a puppy dog, I nearly pissed myself." He went to Pete and slapped him on the back and said, "Nice one, Leroy."

Miller said, "We're in the middle of a very serious discussion, Terzick."

"Oh, right. I'll sit down and fold my hands and be a good little boy." Cobb dropped into a chair. He said, "Do I take it that Moro is no longer suspected of working for a dark power?"

But it wasn't Miller that answered, it was Pete and he said, loud, "We were talking about money."

The others looked surprised and so was I.

Pete said, "And I've got two more things to say on that subject."

Miller looked angry again but Fred said, "Go on, Lieutenant."

"As I understand it, Fred," Pete said, "the current plan is for me and Mr. Moro to tell Billy Sigra that we've killed 'Cobb.' There will be stories in the newspapers and on TV about Cobb's murder. Am I right so far?"

In his chair Cobb acted scared, but Fred said, "Go on."

Pete said, "Since Sigra wouldn't bite on doing the job himself, the idea now is for me to ingratiate myself and get close to Sigra, hoping to discover something incriminating. Do I have the gist of the plan, Fred? Captain?"

"Say what you have to say," Miller said.

"Well, my point is that I need Mr. Moro to do my part convincingly, but Mr. Moro will need you to make it financially worth his while."

And suddenly everybody was looking at me again.

Miller said, "We always intended to give him something."

Fred said, "*If* he was to be an active participant."

Pete said, "By helping me gather information you can use against Billy Sigra Mr. Moro will be in danger for the rest of his life. It'll also affect his earning power. What you pay him has to reflect those facts."

Miller said, "Is this a fucking salary negotiation now?"

Fred said, "What did you have in mind, Mr. Moro?"

Pete said, "Enough money to set himself up and get a permanent place to live."

"How much?" Fred said.

"What do you think, Jan?" Pete said. "Hundred thousand bucks? Two hundred thousand?"

"Don't be fucking ridiculous," Miller said.

"I'm not," Pete said, and he waved his finger, "because money's not a problem, is it, Fred?" We all looked at Fred. "Because that's the second thing I've got to say. I've worked out what Fred's doing here and why he gets to say yes and no. It comes down to money, doesn't it, Fred? It comes down to cash."

Fred said, "Does it?"

"Money flows like dogshit for Operation Judgment Day. Premises and equipment and man-hours and overtime. Because Loftus Pharmaceuticals is picking up the tab. And they're doing that because Billy Sigra is getting in the way of Loftus business plans in South America. So Loftus has got IPD doing its dirty work of getting Billy Sigra out of the way. The truth of the matter is that this real-life police operation has got itself a commercial sponsor. Just like if it was on TV."

Pete stood up. "So there'll be plenty of money for my buddy Jan, commensurate with the fact that he's risking his life to help the business interests of our international drug company sponsor, all purely for justice and truth and the American way, of course." Pete turned to me. "Come on, runt."

I jumped up.

"Sit down, Powder," Miller said.

But Pete didn't sit down, even when Miller said it again and ordered him. Pete just walked out of the room and down the passage to outdoors, and I followed him and nobody stopped us.

On the way to the car I said, "Where are we going?"

"Someplace I can cool down."

He was mad with Miller and Fred but even so I said, "Are they really going to pay me two hundred thousand dollars?"

But before Pete could answer a black sports car roared up and squealed to a stop behind Pete's own car. The driver jumped out and said, "Is the meeting over? Have I missed it?"

Pete said, "Naw. There's still plenty of shit in the stew."

The man didn't know how to take that, but he walked towards us around his car and when he did that, I realized I knew him. I couldn't believe it! I tugged at Pete's sleeve, but Pete shook me off when the guy stuck his hand out and said, "Major López Oso. And you would be?"

Pete said, "I would be a movie star with a mansion in Florida, but who I am is Lieutenant Leroy Powder."

"Ah!" the Major guy said, and he raised his hands like he was excited. "The redoubtable Lieutenant Powder! It is a pleasure to meet you at last."

Pete turned to me and said, "See, runt? A fan club."

The Major guy turned to me and I could tell he recognized me. He said, "And is this your . . . assistant?"

"He sure as hell is," Pete said. "Allow me to introduce Jan Moro, who is the meanest, most dangerous son of a bitch in the whole of Indianapolis. I'm a pussycat compared to Madman Moro. Don't you *ever* get him riled, not if you value your *cojónes*. I saw him in action just this afternoon, and Madman Moro is *bad*."

The Major guy looked at Madman Moro in a completely different way from how he looked at Pete's assistant. "A very great pleasure to meet you, Mr. Madman."

So I did my best to look *bad* because if Pete was going to get me all that money I didn't want to let him down.

Then the Major guy said to Pete, "But if the meeting continues why are you leaving?"

"Because I can't stand listening to them anymore."

"Ah, a man of action, not talk."

"You could say that."

"With them it is all talk talk talk, eh?"

"I'm not real happy with *what* they say either," Pete said.

The Major guy said, "I know exactly what you mean. Everything for them is so slow, they make it all so hard. I tell them it is simple to set a trap. All you need is good bait. But they cluck like old men and tell me, 'We couldn't do things like that here.' In my country we are more direct."

"Yeah?"

"And between you and me, Lieutenant Powder, my patience is sorely tried. Time runs out, and waits for no man, eh? Doing nothing is not the way to solve one's problems."

But before Pete said anything to that, from behind us Miller said, "You coming in here to get down to business, Ramón, or you planning to shoot the breeze with those two assholes all day long?"

30.

Pete didn't say anything when we got in the car, but he slammed the door and he screeched his tires and suddenly everything he did was hard and he was halfway to scaring me again.

While we waited for traffic I said, "That guy we were just talking to? I know him." But Pete didn't pay any attention. He pulled out fast into a gap and then he banged his fist on the dashboard.

So I looked out the window for a while. What I felt like was going out to where there were race cars running, because I sure could use the sound of those big engines to help me understand everything that was happening.

It was getting more and more confused. The latest thing was Major López Oso, who I knew because he was Ramón. The same Ramón who was talking like a pal to Billy Cigar, with Barb there as the loose woman. The same Ramón who called

Barb on the phone in the morning and who upset her and who she was doing some kind of job for.

And on top of all that, seeing Ramón suddenly reminded me that it was hours since I left Barb in her car waiting outside the Linger Longer Lounge. She couldn't still be there, could she? Not after all this time. Could she?

Finally I couldn't stay quiet anymore. I said, "Where are we going?"

Pete said, "To hell in a drug company hand basket."

Well, I didn't know what that was supposed to mean except he was still angry. I said, "Look, can you stop and let me out. There's someplace I've got to go."

"Since when?"

"There's a friend I've got to see if she's home."

"For Christ's sake, runt, she's in the goddamn hospital in Chicago."

"Not Rosie," I said. "Another friend. I need to see if she's O.K. But you're not in a good mood so why don't you drop me and then we can meet up again later on." Pete didn't say anything for nearly two blocks. I said, "Can you stop and let me off, please?"

I was thinking about whether I could jump out of the car at the next light when Pete said, "You agreed to work with me. You're not quitting now."

"I thought you didn't like what Miller and Fred want us to do."

"I don't. It stinks. It's corrupt. It's contrary to everything I've always worked for as a policeman."

"But are you still going to do it?"

"I don't fucking know," he said. "I've got to think it through."

"You mean I still might get my two hundred thousand bucks?"

"Don't spend it yet, runt. It's what we call a bargaining position."

"So how much will they give me?"

"I don't know," he said.

"One hundred thousand?" But he didn't say anything. I said, "I'd take fifty thousand, if you thought that was fair." But he was definitely not talking about it. I said, "So are you going to let me off, or what?"

"If you think I'm letting you out of my sight now, you're crazy." But then he said, "Tell me where you want to go."

So I directed him to Barb's house.

Barb's car wasn't in the driveway and her place was dark even though a lot of her neighbors had their lights on.

"Nobody's home," Pete said.

"I want to look through the windows."

"So look," he said. But he came with me and we looked together.

And, for sure, Barb wasn't there. When we came back to the car I said, "There's someplace else I've got to go." I thought he might get mad again so I said, "I can walk. I don't mind."

But he just said, "Where?"

"Billy's club."

"Is that some kind of dwarfish joke?"

"My friend, she gave me a ride down there this morning. She might still be waiting outside."

"Since this morning? This friend got a serious IQ problem?" But he started the car.

After a while Pete said, "Tell me something."

"What?"

"Is it true, what they say? That short guys have more fun? How many lady friends you got scattered around this town, runt? One in every neighborhood?"

That reminded me of a story a guy told me in a bar one time. It was about this priest and this rabbi who were having a discussion.

The priest said to the rabbi, "Tell me something."

"Sure," the rabbi said. "What do you want to know?"

"Whenever I have bacon," the priest said, "I feel really sorry for you Jewish guys because you never get to have it, do you?"

"No," the rabbi said. "We don't eat bacon."

"But there must have been a time," the priest said, "before you became a rabbi. Then, just the once, didn't you want to try bacon? To see what you were missing."

"To tell you the truth," the rabbi said, "there was one time. I was young. I thought, what can it hurt? And I had a bacon sandwich."

"Great, wasn't it?" the priest said. "Isn't that just about the best taste you can imagine?"

"Yes, it was good," the rabbi said. "I admit it was good." And then the rabbi said, "May I ask you something now, Father?"

"Of course, of course."

"There must have been a time, before you were ordained, there must have been a time when you really wanted to know what you'd be missing when you gave up women."

"To tell you the truth," the priest said, "there was a time like that. I had this urge, and I went out, and—just the once—I slept with a woman."

And the rabbi said, "It's a hell of a lot better than bacon, am I right?"

Barb's car was still parked out front of the Linger Longer, only she wasn't inside. Pete stopped behind it, but he left the motor running.

"O.K.? You satisfied?"

"She's probably in the club. I want to go and look for her."

Pete signaled to pull back into traffic. "You thought she might be waiting in the car. She's not waiting in the car. So she found a better way to pass the time. Maybe she's singing the national anthem for the Pacers or maybe she's pulling a train somewhere. But you are not going into the Linger Longer to look for her."

I said, "My stuff is in her car."

"What stuff?"

"Everything. My sleeping bag. All my clothes."

He scratched at his beard and then he turned off the engine. We got out and went to Barb's car, but the doors were locked.

Pete said, "I don't see any sleeping bag."

"Try the trunk. She probably moved everything there so nobody would steal it."

He tried the trunk, but that was locked too. He said, "We're not going to break it open, runt."

"That's why I want to go into the club. That's where she'd look for me."

"Well she won't find you there, will she?"

"But why hasn't she come out again?"

"If you're so worried about her, leave a note on the windshield."

But I didn't want to do that. "What about my sleeping bag?"

"You won't need a sleeping bag tonight."

"But I'll need clothes. My shirt's ripped."

"I'll buy you some goddamned clothes. Now get back in the car or I'll break both your fucking legs."

We drove south till he found a mall, but when we'd parked I didn't feel like getting out.

Pete said, "Stop sulking. By the time we're through you'll look like you came straight out of a K mart catalogue."

"I don't want new clothes. I want to know Barb's O.K."

"Tough," he said. " 'Cause we're not going to the Linger Longer."

"Why not?"

"We got someplace else to go."

"Where?"

"You'll see."

I said, "Can we go to the Linger Longer after that?"

He was quiet for a moment. Then he said, "Maybe, later. I

suppose we could have a drink and show the world what great pals we are."

And I could tell when he said it that however much he hated Miller and Fred he still might carry on working for them and so I still had an outside chance for my fifty thousand.

31.

When Pete drove out of the mall we went underneath an Interstate and into a residential area. After a while he turned up the driveway of a one-story white house. The driveway was different from the rest in the neighborhood because it rose gradually to a couple of feet above yard level. Then, around the back, it broadened into space for several cars and there was a concrete lip that ran straight to the back door, without steps or a porch.

One car was already there and I didn't know whether it was another meeting we were going to. Pete parked and then he got out and went to the back door. I got out too and was following behind when he started pounding on the door and shouting, "Open up! Police!"

It made me wonder what I was doing there.

The door opened, and it was Sergeant Fleetwood in a

wheelchair. She saw it was Pete and she said, "What are *you* doing here?"

He said, "Do you know, do you have the slightest idea what pretty boy Proffitt has got me and my pal Moro involved in?"

"Don't play games, Roy Powder. Either tell me what you want or go away." She sounded tired and she also sounded like she was talking to a kid.

Although she only said it in a normal voice Pete stopped like he'd been shouted at. He looked at her and then he said, "Sorry. I seem to make the most fuss when I'm least sure of myself."

Sergeant Fleetwood shook her head slowly. She said, "I hardly hear from you, for months."

"Ah, but, see, the dog and hog—"

"Then, in one day, you disrupt my office, you call me, and you show up on my doorstep uninvited. And no doubt you expect me to say, 'Come in, sit down, have a cup of coffee, let me hold your hand,' as if everything is just the way it used to be."

"I am sorry," Pete said.

"So what *do* you want?"

"To come in, sit down, drink coffee and have my hand held."

She began to close the door.

"Wait! I'd like to do some sewing. And I want your advice about a moral dilemma."

She didn't say anything, but she stopped closing the door.

He said, "I can talk morality and sew at the same time."

"What sewing?"

"I tore Moro's shirt this morning. He won't let me buy a new one, so I want to mend it. I'll get a better color match for the thread from your sewing basket. Mine only has black and white and his shirt is gray."

"Half an hour," she said.

"Half an hour."

She rolled back and I followed Pete in.

* * *

Sergeant Fleetwood's kitchen had a lot of space in the middle and a table top hanging down from the wall like a flap. Right away it was a place I was comfortable in. What I liked best was that everything was lower than in a usual kitchen—the stove, the sink, the level of the table, everything. It felt inviting, and it reminded me of the trusting feeling I'd had about Sergeant Fleetwood, even though she was a cop.

There was only one chair and she didn't say to sit down so I waited and what happened was that Pete said, "Let me have your shirt."

"What?"

"Your shirt."

"It's O.K. the way it is," I said.

"I'm not going to any club tonight with a guy who flashes flesh through holes in his shirt."

"Are we going to the club?"

"I just said so, didn't I?"

Well, it was a promise and there was a witness. I turned my back and took my shirt off. Then I pulled my jacket around to cover up as best I could.

From a drawer Sergeant Fleetwood took out a box with embroidery all over it. Pete hunted through the spools of thread and he looked like he knew what he was doing. At the same time he said, "Did Homer Proffitt tell you that Loftus Pharmaceuticals is *paying* for Operation Judgment Day?"

"No," Sergeant Fleetwood said.

"And that Loftus is calling the tune? And that the reason for targeting Billy Sigra is that he's an obstacle to Loftus business down where Sigra killed all those people. Do you have a bigger thimble somewhere?"

Pete sewing reminded me of the one good thing when all us kids and Momma went to visit Momma's parents the time I got to know the pigs. The good thing was a sewing machine in the house and it had a foot pedal and the pedal made a wheel go around. I played for hours with the pedal and the wheel. Like, I'd take an egg beater and hold it up against the wheel so by pushing the sewing machine pedal I made the egg beater beat. Only then Momma's momma got mad and told me to keep out of her kitchen drawers.

"What?"

"See," Pete said. "He goes off into another world sometimes."

"He did the same when he was in my office," Sergeant Fleetwood said.

"Moro," Pete said, "I just asked Carollee if you could use her shower and she said you could. You want to take a shower while she and I talk?"

Sergeant Fleetwood said, "There's plenty of hot water. Shall I show you where it is?"

Life's like that. You can go three months without a shower and then twice in the same day you get a shower and hot water and soap and towels and everything.

It reminded me of a story a guy told me in a bar once. "I'm the greatest comedian in the whole world," he said to me.

"Oh yeah?" I said.

"I'm the greatest goddamn comedian in the whole world. I'm the Great Rinaldi. And do you want to know the secret of my success?"

"I never heard of you," I said. I thought maybe he was going to tell me that his success was the secret.

But he said, "You got a honest face. You want to know the secret of my success, all you got to do is ask."

"O.K. What?"

"No, you got to ask. Ask me, 'Great Rinaldi, the greatest comedian in the whole goddamn world, what is the secret of your success?' Ask me that."

"Rinaldi—"

"No no. 'Great Rinaldi.' "

"Great Rinaldi, the greatest comedian in the whole god-damn world, what is the secret of—"

"Timing!" he said.

The shower felt good, but I started thinking about Barb and how her car was still where it was when she let me out in the morning. Of course she might have gone someplace else, but most likely she went into the Linger Longer looking for me and found Billy instead.

Before, Billy was just a name. He was a guy who bought people drinks and told stories and seemed like a person to try the slow-release deodorant on.

But now he himself had told me about blowing a guy's brains out all over his shirt. So he was not a person I wanted Barb to have any business with.

She might say it was none of my never-mind, but the least I could do was tell her about Billy so's she could decide for herself.

Then I thought about my things in her trunk. If I have my sleeping bag and file with me, I don't worry where I'm going to sleep at night because I can bed down most anywhere, but without them I had to be a lot more—

"You going to spend all night in here?"

"What?"

I looked out between the shower curtains and I saw that Pete had opened the bathroom door and come in.

He picked up my clothes.

"Hey, put those down!" I said.

"Carollee's going to let me press all your stuff. Got to look sharp if we're gonna party." He laid a pink bathrobe on the toilet seat and on top of that he put a pair of slippers. The slippers had bunny ears and faces. "You're gonna be lovely," he said.

When I came out, Pete was busy at an ironing board with Sergeant Fleetwood watching.

Pete said, "Carollee thinks we should see the Sigra operation through and complain afterwards. She thinks Miller will have my ass hauled up in front of a disciplinary hearing if I quit now."

"Oh," I said.

"She also thinks sticking with it is your best chance at ending up with some cash. So how does that sound? You willing to go after Billy Sigra with me?"

"O.K.," I said. "Can I have my clothes now?"

"No," Pete said.

Sergeant Fleetwood said, "Was the shower all right?"

"Fine."

"By the way, Mr. Moro, your friend Rose is in Cook County General Hospital in Chicago, but I won't have a report on how she's doing until probably Monday."

"Cook County," I said. "Thanks."

"Something else I've learned about our friend Moro," Pete said. "He's a hell of a ladies' man."

"Yeah?" Sergeant Fleetwood said.

"It's the bunny slippers that drives 'em wild."

32.

We left Sergeant Fleetwood's only a couple of minutes after the half hour was up. Pete did an O.K. job on mending my shirt but even ironed it didn't feel like it did when it was brand-new.

"Now," he said, "we catch something to eat."

"You said we'd go to the Linger Longer."

"Too early."

"I'm not hungry."

"You can watch me eat."

I didn't say anything to that because there was no point in aggravating him while I still had a chance for my fifty thousand bucks.

Of course probably what would happen was I would help them out but they wouldn't pay up, even ten or twenty. And there wouldn't be anything I could do about it, because someone like me would never win with a lawyer against the police.

I remembered a story I heard in a bar one time. This guy said, "They ought to do laboratory experiments on lawyers instead of rats."

We all looked around at each other, but the guy said, "No, really. It makes sense."

"How's that?" somebody said.

"In the first place, there's a lot more lawyers than there are rats. And in the second place, it's possible to feel affection for a rat."

Pete must have known in his mind where he wanted to eat because we passed lots of restaurants before we stopped and then it was only a small place and not fast food at all. When we walked in, all the restaurant people seemed to know him like he was an old friend and what he ordered was a pizza without even looking at the menu.

I had a beer and while Pete was shaking hands and talking I got to wondering how much attention he would really pay to what Sergeant Fleetwood said about my money, now we weren't sitting in her house. I figured it depended how badly Pete wanted to make her feel good by saying he took her advice.

So when he settled down at the table I said, "Is it true you didn't see Sergeant Fleetwood for a long time like she said?"

"What's it to you, runt?"

"I just wondered why," I said, "because this afternoon you said you liked her a lot. Or was that not true?"

I thought maybe he'd start to talk about her, but what happened was a moment of meanness passed through his face, and then he got a faraway look.

I nursed my beer and wondered if I really did have a chance for all that money. That got me to thinking about a guy I used to know. He was a heavy drinker and more than once he ended up in the drunk tank of whatever city he was in.

Well, he told me about this one place where they put the drunks into a wire cage in the corner of the courtroom and the night court judge would come into the room and hear the cases then and there, right in front of the cage.

Well, one night, the guy said, he was in the cage and the night court judge was judging away, fifteen days for this one, thirty days for that one when suddenly he hears the judge tell some guy, "I've listened to your story, and I've decided to give you a second chance."

"When I heard that," the guy told me, "I hit the cage wire like a runaway truck. I climbed up and I started shouting, 'I'll have one of those too, Your Honor. I'll have one of those!' "

"Carollee is my heart's shaman," Pete said.

"What?"

"You asked me a question."

"Oh. Right."

But that's when the pizza came.

After we left the restaurant even then it wasn't the Linger Longer we went to. Pete drove to a motel.

"What are we doing here?" I said.

"Getting you a place to sleep."

"I'm not tired."

"But you do get tired, don't you? Or do you spend your nights going from house to house, woman to woman?"

In the motel office a pale guy who looked middle-aged was frowning and squinting at a TV set. When he realized we were there he stood up. "Can I help you fellas?"

Pete said, "We want a single room."

"Single, you say?"

"Single I say," Pete said.

The man looked from one of us to the other, but then he put a card down on the counter. "Fill it out."

Pete pushed the card to me, but I said, "You're paying for it," so Pete filled the card out himself.

The man turned it around and bent down to look at it. "It's unit twenty-three, Mr . . . Uh, is that 'Stark' or 'Starch'?"

"Moro," I said.

"Starch," Pete said.

"Pay in advance," the guy said.

Outside the office Pete said, "You want to look at your room or shall we go straight to the Linger Longer?"

"The Linger Longer," I said so we got back in his car.

"You ever stayed in a motel before?"

"Sure," I said. "Lots of times."

Pete laughed.

"It's true!" I said, and it was, from when I lived in Detroit and part of my work needed traveling, though I try to forget those days now.

But the first time I stayed in a motel was while Daddy was on trial. We needed the motel because they had to do his fair trial in Lafayette instead of Indy, because of bad things the Indy newspaper said about Daddy when he got caught.

It was the newspaper that paid for the room. Daddy's lawyer said the only reason they paid for me and Cissy and Wayne to be there was so it would look like they were nice guys. But the "nice guys" still said Daddy ought to get the maximum conviction, even though he never meant to shoot. They said Daddy didn't show remorse because he wouldn't rat on the two guys who did the shooting with him, only Daddy didn't even know who they were because of the masks, but nobody believed him.

All us kids went to the court each day, but I don't remember everything that happened real well. What I do recall is two things. One was that when I went outside, people would ask me what I felt like, but I didn't know what to feel. The other was that in the court, Daddy cried and I don't know how much more remorse a guy can show than that.

"What?"

"We're here."

And then I could see he meant the club.

Barb's car was still where it was. We drove past it and parked outside the Chinese restaurant across the next street.

Pete said, "I know you want to find out what happened to your little girlfriend, but what we're here for is to show what great buddies we are."

"O.K."

"And if we see Sigra we laugh at his jokes and pay attention to what he says."

"Do you know yet how much money they're going to pay me?"

"No," Pete said, and he sounded mad I asked, though it seemed a reasonable question to me. "Concentrate," he said. "We've got to remember as much of what Sigra says as we can."

"Yeah, all right."

"In a normal undercover operation, we'd be wearing wires. Transmitters, so that guys outside could hear everything and tape it."

"But we don't get that?"

"Miller thinks Sigra is too dangerous to wear wires with. We might get stripped and searched."

And it was true that when I went to talk to Linda one of Billy's guys patted me down before I went in and he did a good job, though he didn't strip me. I said, "You'd think in this day and age they'd have wires that wouldn't show."

"Wouldn't show when you're standing in your birthday suit?"

"How about ones that are microchips, or ones that they could put under your skin?"

Pete raised his eyebrows after I said that. "Surgically implanted transmitters, huh? Body wires. That's not a bad idea, runt."

"I get lots of ideas," I said, and I began to think if Pete liked the idea about a body wire, maybe later he would tell me someone at the cops I could sell it to.

33.

The guy on the door at the club was Ed again. When Pete and I passed him I said, "Hi, Ed," but he looked at me like I was out of Dracula's basement and didn't say anything back.

Then we came to a guy in a cowboy hat. He stopped us and said, "Two?"

Pete said, "Is there a problem?"

"You guys want a table? You going to have a meal?"

"We'll sit at the bar and leave the tables for canasta," Pete said.

"That'll be seven bucks each," the guy said.

"Is it cheaper if we eat something?"

"Is that supposed to be funny?"

"What's the charge for?" Pete said.

"The Prairie Dogs."

"The what?"

"The band."

"Oh, fuck," Pete said.

The guy said, "We have a band in here most every Saturday night. We're famous for it."

"Haven't you heard of silence?" Pete said. "In California they proved if you make it real quiet, people drink faster and clubs make more money."

"Silence you can have outside. In here we got the Prairie Dogs," the guy said.

Pete paid him and we went in.

I followed Pete to the part of the bar furthest away from the entrance. It was next to the combination lock door, and near the toilets, and it was a good spot to watch the rest of the lounge, which was pretty full considering how early it was.

Pete said, "You want help getting onto the stool, little fella?" but it was only a joke and he called to the barman and ordered a couple of beers.

I couldn't see Barb anywhere. Or Billy.

We didn't talk. We just drank and looked around, but a couple of times Pete slapped me on the back and laughed like I'd told him something funny. Then after a while the lights went down, and a guy came out and introduced himself as the emcee and he started telling stories. They were the crude kind, which is not my taste, but after each one Pete hit his knee and laughed longer than anybody else in the place.

Then the guy introduced a band, but it wasn't the Prairie Dogs. It was the Four Six-Guns and it had three guys who looked like hippies in cowboy suits and a girl singer.

I liked her but Pete twisted a lot on his stool during the first number, so it surprised me when at the end of the song he clapped and whistled and stomped. When she started singing her next song Pete leaned towards me and said, "I thought Sigra was supposed to like this crap. So where is he?" But before I could answer he sat up again and whooped.

It was then I saw Ramón come in. I tugged Pete's arm and pointed Ramón out.

"What the fuck is *he* doing here?" Pete said. And then he whispered, "According to Miller, everybody but us is supposed to keep a mile away from this joint."

"That can't be right," I said. "I saw Ramón in here two nights ago."

"The hell you did," Pete said, and then he hit me on the shoulder, hard, and he laughed.

"Hey, cut that out!"

The bartender came up to get our glasses. Pete said, "Same again for my buddy and me," and the bartender nodded and went away.

Then Pete said, "López Oso was in here the night before last?"

"Yeah. Him and these two women were talking to Billy at the bar." I tried to point out where, which was near the other end of the horseshoe, but Pete hit me on the shoulder again. "You're a caution!" he said.

"Stop hitting me!".

The bartender put two bottles down and Pete paid him and then he said to me, "López Oso was talking to *Sigra*?"

"Yeah."

Pete looked Ramón's way. "What the fuck is he up to?"

"I don't know," I said.

"Whatever it is," Pete said, "I'll bet you a prairie dog Miller doesn't know anything about it. Did you hear what they were talking about?"

"Billy was telling about how one time when he was a cop he came home and found another cop there with his wife, and Billy lit out after the guy and there was some shooting only nobody got hurt and in the end the other guy got suspended but Billy had to quit."

"Just what was López Oso's part in this conversation?"

"He introduced Billy to one of the women."

"Introduced? You mean fixed him up?"

"He thought they might like each other."

"And did they?"

"Yeah."

Just then the bartender passed by and Pete said to him, "Is Billy around?"

"Maybe later."

"He doesn't like the music, huh?" Pete said.

"He loves it," the bartender said. "He's usually here to greet the band, but he had some late business come up."

I said, "Have you seen a woman with blond hair that's all in little curls, and wearing a red dress?"

The bartender said, "If you already know all about it, then why ask me?" and he went away.

Pete turned my way slowly and I didn't like the expression on his face.

"What?" I said.

"Your friend?"

"Yeah."

"With Sigra?"

"I guess."

He scratched at his beard and looked for all the world like he was tired of life. "Is it supposed to be a coincidence, that they're together?"

"How do I know? Last time I saw her she was waiting for me in the car." But the way Pete kept staring made me remember about how he said I'd better not let him down.

Then he hit me on the shoulder again and laughed. "Drink up, little buddy. We're going to go out and get some peace and quiet."

34.

In the car outside the Chinese restaurant Pete said, "I want the story on your friend, runt."

"Why?"

"Start with her name. Now."

"Barb."

"How long have you known her?"

"Not long. Look, what's all the—"

"How did you meet her?"

I said, "I don't see why I have to answer questions when I may not get paid anything at all."

Speaking slow and low and mean, Pete said, "How did you meet Barb?"

It was a time to go with the flow. I said, "She was with that Ramón guy the other night."

"With him?" Pete said. "You mean she was the woman López Oso introduced to Sigra?"

"That's right."

"So, how does she come to be *your* friend?"

"Last night I went back to the club and she was there and she tapped me on the shoulder and she thought I might know where Billy was but I didn't, and then we got to talking."

Pete thought about that. "So, how is it she drove you here this morning?"

"I slept on her couch last night."

"You slept at her house?"

"Yeah."

"If she was looking for Sigra last night, does that mean she was still looking for him this morning?"

"Yeah," I said.

"Yet she didn't know him at all till two days ago?"

"That's right." But then I thought about the pictures of Billy that Barb had on the table in her house when I came in, and how she was doing some kind of job for Ramón.

Pete said, "Why was she trying to find Sigra?"

I didn't want to say.

"Runt, why was this woman looking so hard for Billy Sigra?"

But I had to. "She had some kind of job with him, something Ramón hired her for. But I don't think she should do it, because Billy is a real bad guy and that's why I want to find her and warn her about him."

Pete sat thinking.

I said, "You better make sure they pay me."

Pete said, "Where we stopped this afternoon, that's Barb's house?"

"Yeah."

"And last night, you left the club with her?"

"Yeah, but first she drove me out to the Fairgrounds, to pick up my sleeping bag and stuff. That's when you and Miller chased me. And you did chase me, you did!"

"Where did you and Barb go then?"

"We went back to her place." I remembered something. "Only . . ."

"Only what?"

"She stopped to make a phone call. When she decided I could sleep over she said, 'I'm going to have to make a phone call.' "

"Who to?"

"I don't know, but she talked for a long time."

"And then you went to her house?"

"Yeah."

"And while you were there did she say anything else about Sigra or López Oso?"

"Ramón called up this morning and Barb talked Spanish to him and some of it was angry."

"She knows Spanish?"

"Yeah, and she talks it fast."

"What did she say?"

"How do I know? Except I heard her say Ramón's name."

"And what happened after that?"

"We had breakfast and then she drove me here. I went to look in the club to see if Billy was there and I was going to come back out and tell her, only instead I ran into you."

"So, when you didn't come back she went into the Linger Longer looking for Sigra herself?"

"I guess so."

"And she found him," Pete said, which he heard the bartender say as well as I did. "So, we've got a Spanish-speaking mystery woman who works for López Oso, who gets introduced to Sigra and who finds him today. And then suddenly Sigra doesn't show up for the Saturday night music show. It's beginning to sound like she might be quite a gal, your friend Barb. I begin to wonder who ought to be warned about who."

"You don't think that—"

"I'm going to call Miller now, runt. I'm going to tell him

what López Oso is up to. I'm going to enjoy telling Miller about his good buddy who gets impatient with all the talk, talk, talk."

"O.K.," I said.

"But if you go anywhere while I'm gone, you're dead."

Pete got out of the car and went into the Chinese restaurant and they must have had a phone in there because Pete stayed a long time.

When he came back, first thing he did was start up the car. Then he said, "It's hitting the fan now, runt. Miller's getting Proffitt and Feske together and we're going to have a meeting."

"Yeah?"

"You've got two choices now. One of them is to go back to your motel."

"Yeah, I'll do that."

"But you stay put."

"Sure," I said. "Where would I go?"

35.

Pete didn't talk while we drove, and that was O.K. by me because I was thinking over and over about his idea that Barb might be *dangerous*. That had never once crossed my mind before, but I could see how it fit with the things I'd told Pete about her.

Even so, when I thought through the time I'd spent with Barb, I couldn't remember a single thing she said or did that scared me. Myself, I've never once known a woman who was dangerous the way Pete thought Barb might be for Billy, even though guys in bars are forever saying about women, "She's killing me!" I always take that for a joke, but I suppose it could happen, and you see it on television sometimes, about women killing people, even if it's usually the other way around.

The baddest woman I ever knew personally was Gloria, but I'd never call her a killer even though sometimes she said she'd like to kill us kids. But it *was* because of Gloria that Daddy got into his trouble. I can see a lot better how it came about now that I'm older. Daddy kept needing more and more money for buying Gloria presents and for trying to make her say, "Oh Clarence! Is that for me?" in that whispery, giggly voice she put on when she was saying thank you, though I *never* believed she was truly thankful.

The way Daddy went crazy over Gloria taught me things for the rest of my life and I have tried never to get that way over a woman myself.

In bars I've also heard guys tell about the stupid things they've done for the love of women, even when they were more than old enough to know better. Some old guys act like they were still teenagers but when you point it out they say they can't help themselves. I wouldn't call them liars, but yourself is just about the only person who ever *can* help you, so it's hard for me to know what makes guys like that tick.

Despite all the perfume and bracelets and silver compacts, Gloria never even came to Daddy's trial, not one time. Daddy looked around the trial audience every day, and I knew it could only be her that he was looking for, because he always knew where Wayne and Cissy and me were sitting.

"What?"

But I could see what. We were at the motel and the car was stopped outside the room I had the key for in my pocket.

Pete said, "If I get a chance, I'll ask Miller about your money, maybe get him to pay an installment."

"How much?"

"I don't know, but suppose I pick you up about eight and take you out for breakfast. I can tell you about it then."

"O.K.," I said.

"Sweet dreams," he said and I got out and went into the motel room.

* * *

When I got inside and turned on the light I could hardly believe that it was all for me. There was this enormous bed and a TV and a telephone and an armchair and a carpet on the floor and a clock. I patted the bed, and the spread on it was shiny and smooth and cool. I said, "Wow!" right out loud, even though there was nobody to say it to and talking to yourself is supposed to be crazy. It just slipped out and I couldn't help myself.

And when I walked around the room I found there was more, a whole bathroom, and it even had soap and a hair dryer and a matchbook that when I opened it up turned out to be a little sewing kit. I flushed the toilet and I tried the shower and I turned on the hair dryer and everything worked and I still couldn't hardly believe it all.

Then I went back to the main room and I sat down on the armchair. I took my shoes off and I wiggled my toes in the carpet. And I took off all my clothes. I was going to lay them on the floor, but I noticed a door that I hadn't tried and it turned out to be a closet with hangers so I put my clothes in there.

What I did after that was stretch out on the bed. The bedspread's cool, satiny feel was amazing on my skin. I rolled myself up in the bedspread and I wiggled around just feeling it.

After a while I unrolled and went over to the TV. I couldn't see how to turn it on, so I started pushing buttons, and when I got the right one the TV almost jumped off the rack as it came alive. The program was Roseanne saying, "What do *I* do about contraception? I go in the bedroom and I just take another look at my kids."

I went back and rolled up in the bedspread again, and I lay like that watching the TV for a long, long time.

Finally, about a quarter to eleven, it felt like I'd waited long enough so I got dressed and went out.

36.

Barb's car was still outside the Linger Longer and I stood looking at the trunk for a minute, and I thought about breaking in to get my stuff out. But I wasn't sure that was the right plan, especially while people were still going in and out of the club and might get the wrong idea of what I was doing. So I decided to wait inside the club until it closed. That could be good in another way too because maybe meanwhile somebody would say something about Billy and where he was or what happened to him.

I could have gone in the club by the front again, but I didn't see any point to spending seven bucks that was mine if the guy in the cowboy hat didn't remember me. So I headed around the side.

From the morning I knew where Billy's office was and I got the idea to listen through the window and see what I could hear.

I kept to the shadows and didn't hurry and when I got there at first I couldn't hear anything, but then I heard a woman's voice.

For just a moment I thought it was Barb and my heart raced because it meant Pete was wrong, because if Barb killed Billy she'd never come back to his office. But then I listened some more and I knew it wasn't Barb after all, it was Linda. She was talking to someone on the telephone, but I couldn't hear well enough to know if she was mad or just being bossy, and then she hung up and there was no sound at all for a long time. That made me think she was in the office alone, so I left the window and went to the back door.

The door was unlocked again and like before I slipped in when it seemed quiet and sure enough the corridor was empty. I walked straight into the lounge through the combination door and went into the men's rest room. From there I could hear the music, which didn't have a girl singer so it must be the Prairie Dogs. I relieved myself and washed my hands and checked myself out in the mirror. And then I went back into the main room.

The club was crowded everywhere, even at the end of the bar where Pete and I sat before. I didn't get a stool, but I squeezed in and after a while I caught the barman's eye and I ordered a beer. And then I settled down to listen for a while to the Prairie Dogs.

Maybe when I have my own TV show I'll get booked into clubs too, because of the fame. There was only the one of me instead of the five like the Prairie Dogs, but then they didn't tell jokes, which I had just about decided for sure that I would. I had no idea what money they charged to do a show, but I was bound to be able to do it for less. I got the idea to try to talk to a Prairie Dog later on, as one businessman to another, and make it sound like it wasn't because I was going into competition.

With the big crowd it was hard for me to make out if there was anybody I knew, so after a while I took my beer and I stood against a wall. From there I could see better, and for one thing I could see that Ramón wasn't at the table where I saw him when I was with Pete.

Ramón might have gone home, but it could also be he was somewhere else in the club. And it came into my head, what if I had run into him in the rest room? It could have happened. Even guys from South America pee, and what I liked about the idea was that to Ramón I was Madman Moro. I could have said, "Hey, out of my way," and he would have stepped aside.

Then I could have said, "You shouldn't be here," and I could have waved a finger in his face and said, "Part of the deal with Miller is you're not supposed to come here and you're also not supposed to talk to Billy. Now, you got two seconds flat to make your feeble excuses before I do something to you that's going to *hurt*."

Since he thought I was Madman Moro he'd start talking quick and not say to mind my own business. And I could also say, "Now let's have the story about you and Barb. And don't tell me lies, because it sure doesn't pay to get me riled." He'd remember what Pete said about riling me and he'd get scared and keep talking.

"What?"

I felt a hand on my shoulder. I nearly jumped over the guy standing next to me, and I spilled beer all down my shirt. And then I saw that the hand on my shoulder belonged to Billy Cigar, who was alive and grinning and not dead at all. I stood there shaking, he scared me so bad.

"Hey, shorty," Billy said, "you just wet yourself."

"Yeah," I said and I wiped at it though it didn't do any good.

Meanwhile Billy said, "I hear you and Yount come round earlier. Patched things up, huh?"

"Yeah," I said.

"Look, how you feel about doing me a little favor?"

"A favor? What?"

He took some keys from his pocket and flipped them up in

front of me. I wasn't expecting them, so I didn't catch them and they dropped on the floor close to my feet.

Billy laughed. "Butterfingers," he said.

I picked the keys up and then Billy leaned close and I had the sudden, crazy idea that he was going take a bite out of my ear. But instead all he was really doing was being private. He said, "There's a car parked out front of the club."

"A car?"

"Yellow Ford. I want you to lose it."

"Lose it?"

"Drive it somewhere and leave it. You do know how to drive, don't you?"

"Yeah."

"Anywhere that ain't close to here. Dump it. Come back. I'll give you fifty bucks. Deal?"

I was being paid to lose Barb's car!

"Yes or no?" Billy said. " 'Cause I got things to do."

"Yeah," I said.

"Good."

I stood there.

"So go do it!" Billy said.

37.

When I got to Barb's car, first thing I did was sit inside for a while to get steady. But that wasn't easy because the more I calmed down from Billy scaring me, the more I got worried because though Billy was still alive, Barb was still missing. I knew, though, I couldn't go back in the club and ask Billy what happened to her till I'd moved the car.

I hunted for where to put the key in and then started it up, but I had to hunt some more to get the lights on and to move the seat. Even then the car wouldn't hardly move till I remembered about the parking brake. I know how to drive O.K. but it had been a long time.

When I was a few blocks away from the club and on a dark street I pulled over and stopped. Things in my head were happening too fast. No sooner did I sort out about one thought than

I had another, and this time it was that I couldn't think of a *good* reason why Billy should come back to the club without Barb, but with her keys.

I got out of the car and I went and stood by the trunk. I didn't hurry to unlock it, but on the other hand looking at the outside of a trunk doesn't change what's inside it, which could almost be a philosophy in its own right. So I unlocked the trunk and lifted the lid.

What I found inside was my sleeping bag and my file, and nothing else, and that sure was a relief because I'd been thinking bad thoughts, especially about why Billy wanted me to lose the car for fifty bucks instead of telling one of his own guys who'd do it for free. I left my things where they were and locked up again.

I didn't really want to dump the car just any old where because that would be a pure waste and it also felt like if I abandoned the car I'd abandon Barb. And then I got the idea that maybe the best place for Barb's car would be outside Barb's house.

I found the way but it took near as long as if I'd walked. Streets sure do look different when you're driving, especially if it's not your own car and it matters if you hit stuff. I got faster, though, the longer I went on.

Barb's house was dark when I pulled up out front, but then I had an idea, and this was a good one because it could explain what had happened. The idea was that Barb was inside the house, asleep.

It might be she brought Billy back in the afternoon, driving him in her own car. And then she might have got so tired after their carry-on that she up and went to sleep. It takes some women that way, Rosie for one. With Rosie, she just about always turns over and starts her snoring in two seconds flat, though of course Rosie's a lot older than Barb and not one for stamina.

If that's what happened, then Billy'd need Barb's keys to

drive himself back to the club. And then maybe later on he just wasn't in a good mood and he told me to lose the car because it was hard to explain where to take it back.

With this whole idea in mind I got out and took a closer look at Barb's house. I didn't see lights anywhere or hear any sounds, but that's what you'd expect if she was asleep. I went to the front door and rang the bell a couple times, and when nothing happened to that I tried the handle but the door was locked.

Either Barb wasn't there after all, or she was sleeping real sound. It could be that what I should do was just leave the car and go back to the club and after I got my money I could take the opportunity to ask Billy where Barb was.

But even if I did that, I wasn't sure what was best to do with the keys. I didn't want to leave them in the car itself, because that's stupid and an invitation, but if I hid them someplace then Barb wouldn't know where they were.

In fact it was even possible that Barb herself was back at the club right now. Maybe she woke up and saw the car was gone and had to take a taxi and was hopping mad that the car wasn't where she left it. So I decided that maybe what was for the best was for me to drive the car somewhere close to the club, and that way if I found out where she was I could give her the keys or take the car to her later on.

It was when I went to start the car up that I noticed there was a second key on the ring and it looked like a house key, which made me think it all through again. What I finally did was go to the front door and I tried the key and it worked and that way I got inside Barb's house.

First thing I did was turn some lights on, which showed that the front room was just how we left it in the morning. But even so, Barb could be in her bedroom, sleeping, and though maybe she wouldn't thank me for waking her up I decided I had to look, since I'd gotten this far.

The bedroom door was closed. I knocked hard and waited, but there was no answer so I tried the handle and the door opened right up.

The room was dark and there wasn't enough light from the living room for me to see if she was there or not. I felt along the wall for a light switch, though while I was doing that I decided she wasn't going to be there after all because I couldn't hear her breathing. When Rosie's asleep in a room there's no mistaking it.

I found a switch on the wall but what it turned on was a night-light in a plug just above the baseboard by the door. With that on I could tell where the bed was, though I still couldn't make out for sure if Barb was on it.

I went over to the bed and in the end I felt all over it with my hands, but there was nobody there.

The bed was a really big and firm one and I could have slept sideways in it just as easy as the right way up. Another funny thing, even though we were getting towards the winter there wasn't a single blanket on it, just pillows and sheets. And the sheets were even smoother to the touch than the bedspread back at the motel.

While I sat on the edge of the bed feeling the sheets I worked out that there had to be a way to turn some lights on. No matter who you are or what you're up to, you'll want to see where you threw your clothes when it comes time to put them on again.

I was also beginning to see shapes and outlines where at first everything was just dark. I could tell there was a bureau in the room and it also looked like there were mirrors all across the wall at the foot of the bed end. And then I finally saw some light switches, not in an ordinary place but in the middle of the headboard.

I slid across and turned on the nearest one, but it wasn't light, it was music. The music was a singer I didn't know but the style was a ballad and not bad though ballad's not my own personal taste, so I turned it off. I tried the next switch and that was finally some light, even though it was just a little lamp on the bureau.

What I saw then was how everything in the room was

black, the sheets, the rug, the furniture, even the walls and ceiling, and that's not a common color for a room to be.

The strange thing was that I did know another woman once who had a black bedroom. This was a woman in Detroit called Karen and she had it for her business which was making tapes for VCRs. But a difference was that at Karen's there were places all around the bed for cameras and I didn't see anywhere for a camera in Barb's room.

Karen was real organized with her business and kept a lot of costume clothes and wigs next door so her VCR customers could have exactly what they wanted. Karen could even dress up like different animals, and she had pop star masks, and she had about every kind of uniform you could think of.

I was only there the once, which was to put a pane of one-way glass between the costume room and the black bedroom. Karen's brother helped in her business and he was a pal of the people I worked for in Detroit, and they sent me over to do the glazing, but the glass broke. When Karen's brother got another pane he must have had someone else put it in, because he never called me back even though it wasn't my fault about the first one.

What happened was that the brother came up behind me and tapped me on the shoulder, which was supposed to scare me and make me worry about dropping the glass, but not make me really do it. So I never did get to know Karen very well, though she seemed nice enough from what I saw, and successful in her business, which is always a good sign.

"What? What!"

Out of nowhere I was blinded by bright lights. I didn't know what was happening or what I should do.

Then a voice said, "Good evening."

"Turn those lights off!" I said, but at the same time I rolled from the bed onto the floor.

And then the bright lights went out.

"Who's there? Who's that? What's going on?" I said, but I kept my head down.

The voice said, "It is a comfortable bed, don't you think, *Señor* Madman?"

There was only one guy who called me "Madman." I looked over the edge of the bed and I could see the silhouette of a man standing where the door was open now. I couldn't tell from looking but it had to be Ramón.

I stood up and I said, "What do you think you're doing?"

"I saw the yellow car arrive," he said. "I thought, 'At last the woman has succeeded in bringing Sigra to the house.' "

"You thought I was Billy?"

"The car did not park in the right place so I could not see. But then there was music and light in the bedroom. If it *was* Sigra, I would get no second chance. So, as you see, I entered the house through the back door." He spread his hands shrugging, and it was only then that I saw he was holding a gun.

"You were going to shoot Billy?"

"Of course," he said.

"Why?"

"Because he is evil and killed many people."

"I know," I said, "but—"

"Do you not see the *beauty* of the thing, *Señor* Madman?"

"What beauty?"

Ramón said, "If I kill Sigra and get away to my country, the same law that protects him here protects me there. No extradition. That is beauty, and justice, *no?"*

"You've been setting up with the police to kill Billy?" I said.

"Pah! They are old women, your Captain Miller, your Fred Feske. Fred Feske wishes to do business in my country. But while Billy Sigra walks your streets a free man, it is not possible. So, I am sent here to help your Fred Feske and your Captain Miller take Sigra off the streets. But month after month they accomplish nothing! I cannot stay here forever. So, I make arrangements for myself." Then Ramón looked like he'd just remembered something. He said, "But where is the woman? Is she not here?"

"Billy gave me Barb's keys. Barb and Billy got together this afternoon."

"So I discovered at Sigra's club. That is why I returned here to wait my chance."

"I saw Billy less than an hour ago, but Barb wasn't with him."

"So perhaps he killed her," Ramón said.

"Why would he do *that?*" I said. Not only was it a bad idea, but Ramón made it sound like the natural thing for Billy to do, like maybe blowing his nose.

But Ramón said, "Oh well. I suppose if you and the redoubtable Lieutenant Powder can jail Sigra for the woman's murder that would be sufficient to allow business to progress." He put his gun away. "However, after all the waiting and the talk-talk-talk I had hoped to kill Sigra myself."

From a pocket in his jacket he took out a camera and held it so I could see. "To take a picture of the body," he said with a grin. "Think of it, *Señor* Madman. Myself with the body of Billy Sigra. Think what a hero I would be in my country!"

But I *was* a mad man. The more of Ramón's easy talk about killing I heard, the more riled I got. The camera was the last straw.

I said, "I don't give a *fuck* about your country, and I wouldn't help you put Billy in jail if you paid me!"

I pushed past Ramón and I walked out of the house.

38.

I had trouble driving the car, but this time it was because I was so angry, and the anger didn't get any less the further I drove. In fact it built up, because on top of being mad from thinking about Ramón, I got even madder when I started thinking again about Billy.

At the start Billy'd seemed like a regular guy, buying drinks in the bar and telling stories. Sure, he had what they call a rough edge, but then so do a lot of guys, including my own daddy, who could shout and swear with the best of them if he was in that mood. But I had figured Billy for a guy you could do business with. That's about the best thing I can say about somebody, even though with Billy I always knew I'd need a good way to put my idea to him, whatever it was.

But the more I came to know about Billy Cigar, the more he was a disappointment. I don't like to think bad about people, but Billy was *not* a guy to do business with, there were no two ways about it.

And now, on top of everything else, maybe he'd done something bad to Barb.

"What?"

But it was only a guy honking at me. I couldn't tell why. Probably he just got up on the wrong side of the bed.

I left the car around the corner from the club, on the street where Barb parked it the night she took me home. It seemed forever but it was only the one night ago. Then I walked to the front door and I went in. Ed was gone from under the awning, which was just as well because I was in no mood for small talk.

When I got inside the only music was from a tape and there weren't many people. I spotted Billy right away, where he was sitting at the bar and talking to a fat man with sequins on his shirt.

I walked over and I tapped Billy on the arm. I said, "I want to talk."

He looked down at me and said, "Oh yeah. Wait over by the door to the office."

"I want to talk now."

"You'll get your money when I'm good and ready."

I stood my ground.

Billy gave me a look like I was completely nothing, and that made me even madder, because I may not be much, but I'm *not* nothing. I said, "I don't want your money. I want to know where Barb is."

The fat man said, "Little feller seems to have a hornet up his butt."

"You shut up," I told the fat man. "This is between Billy and me." Billy grabbed for my shoulder but I knocked his hand away. "Where is Barb?"

"Who the fuck is Barb?" he said.

"The woman who owns the yellow car," I said, and I could tell that he knew who I was talking about.

Billy said to the fat man, "Floyd, I apologize for this little peckerwood."

"Shit," Floyd said, "we all got our fleas."

Billy called to a bartender and said, "Y'all give Floyd here whatever he wants."

"That's white of you, Billy," Floyd said.

And then two big guys showed up and stood either side of me. Billy said, "Office."

I tried to shake them off my arms, but they wouldn't let go and they lifted me up and carried me. There was nothing I could do, no matter how mad I was, which was a lesson of its own.

The office was empty when we got to it. Billy closed the door behind us and then all he said was, "Pockets."

Each of the guys was twice my size. I fought them anyhow, but I lost, and they laid what they found on Billy's desk, which was Barb's keys, some money and my motel room key.

Billy picked up the motel key, and he said, "Now how's a little fuck like you get the key to a motel room?"

"Got to sleep somewhere," I said, but before he said anything else I said, "I'm not planning to cause you any trouble, Mr. Cigar. I just want to know where Barb is, that's all."

"You're not going to cause me any trouble, huh?" Billy said.

"That's a promise," I said.

"He's not going to cause me any trouble," Billy said to the two big guys.

They were off to the side standing next to each other and suddenly I got this picture in my head of two big ol' hound dogs, sitting up on their hind legs, tongues out and panting, waiting for a bone.

That made me smile, which Billy didn't like. He said, "You think this is funny?"

"No sir," I said, but I thought about the tongues again and

I couldn't but bust out laughing. I knew it was wrong, but I just had to laugh and laugh, though I kept trying to stop.

It was the last thing in the world Billy was expecting and he didn't know what to do. First he shook his head and said, "There's been some damn thing wrong about you from the start." But then, after a couple of minutes, he got red in the face and said, "*Shut up*!"

I just about bit my tongue off doing it, but I finally stopped laughing.

Billy said to the big guys, "Get rid of him before I do something I regret!"

Each guy took an arm again, but one of them said, "Do you mean, like, kill him, boss?"

"No I don't mean fucking kill him!" Billy shouted. "I mean get rid of him! I never want to see the little fucker again." Then he said to me, "If I *ever* catch you in my club, I'll nail you to the wall and rip the veins out of your arms and stick them in your mouth and let you drown in your own blood," and he turned his back on me, like he was keeping himself from doing it right then and there.

The two big guys carried me out.

My feet didn't touch the ground again until they'd carried me through the parking lot behind the club and down the alley and across a street.

Then one of them said, "Here?"

The other one said, "No. Here is too close." And they picked me up again and carried me down that alley and across another street and into the next alley.

Then they set me down beside some garbage cans and took turns while one of them hit me and the other one held me. I tried to twist and protect myself as best I could, but what saved me most was that they didn't want to hurt their hands or get blood on their clothes. They didn't either one of them really enjoy it.

I got beat up in jail once by a guy who did enjoy it. I

hadn't done anything, just crossed my eyes wrong or something. But that guy sure knew where to hit, and if he skinned his knuckles so much the better. That guy built up scabs on the knuckles of both hands, and he'd reopen the cuts by hitting walls whenever he couldn't get close enough to another con to beat on him. I was in the hospital for a month, and then they put me in solitary for getting into a fight.

"That ought to do it," one of the big guys said.

"Right," the other one said and he let me go and I fell down by the garbage cans.

The first one said, "You heard what Billy's gonna do if he sees you again."

The other one said, "Be smart and don't come back. Billy ain't no guy to be messing with."

The first one said, "Shit, it's starting to rain," and they left me there and set off back to the club like a couple of joggers.

It wasn't hard rain so I decided to stay where I was for a few minutes. I hurt but I knew I was O.K. In fact, I was pretty calm because even while they were still hitting me I had just about decided what I was going to do, once I felt better.

While I lay there a dog came by and it sniffed at me. I reached out but it jumped away. It didn't run though, it backed off, and then it sat down and started to licking itself.

That reminded me of a story a guy in a bar told me one time. It was about two guys walking along the street and they passed an alley and there was a dog in it, licking himself.

The first guy said, "God, I wish *I* could do that!"

The second guy took another look at the dog and then he said, "Well, I think you better pet him first."

After a while I stood up and brushed the dirt and stuff off my clothes. My shirt was ripped again but I could move and breathe all right. I began to walk.

The way I looked at it now I'd gotten just about what I

deserved for being so mad. Not only does it make you stupid, being mad is also no way to do business. I'd gone to Billy and asked him for something when there was nothing for me to offer him back. Being by way of a small businessman myself, I ought to have known better than that. To do a deal you need something to deal with, something to trade.

I headed downtown.

I didn't stop at my closest stash. Instead I went to the City-County Building. Underneath some bushes in one of the raised beds on the south side I dug up the gun I had buried there. And three bullets.

39.

The Linger Longer was the only place I knew to look for Billy Cigar. When I got near, I slowed down and kept to the shadows and I headed straight for the parking lot at the back. It had four cars, though I couldn't be sure that one of them was Billy's.

What I did then was go to Billy's office window. I didn't hear anybody talking inside, but the light was on and that cheered me up about the chance of him still being at the club.

I thought about finding a different dark window to break in, but I decided to try the door at the back of the club first and it was unlocked same as the times before.

I had my gun out and was about to go in when I heard two guys talking, so I found a place behind some trash cans and I waited. What happened was the two guys came through the door and headed for their cars. One guy I recognized as a bartender and the other was one of the big hounds who beat me up.

When I saw him I pointed the gun and went bang bang, though it was only by saying it in my head.

After they each drove away I went to the door and listened again, and this time it was quiet, so I went in. The corridor was clear. What I did was go to Billy's office.

I tried the handle and that door was unlocked too, so I jumped into the room and waved the gun every which way, but the room was empty. I closed the door and I took a look around, and although it was mostly more like a living room than how I think of an office, there was a desk in one corner that had a phone and papers on the top.

I scooped up all the papers and put them in my pocket, which I did out of pure meanness. If what was on them was worth writing down, then my taking them could only cause Billy trouble which was the least I wanted to do to him in case he wasn't still at the club.

I thought maybe I should empty out the desk drawers too but I didn't want Billy to come back and surprise me, so what I did was forget the desk and turn the lights out and hold myself still and ready for when he did come back, if he did.

It seemed like a long, long time till I heard footsteps, but then they stopped outside the office and somebody turned the handle. When the door opened, whoever it was didn't come in at first, maybe surprised it was dark inside. But then he stepped in and reached for the switch and just as the office lights came on the guy's own lights went out because I had a real good shot at the back of his head which is where I hit him with the gun, as hard as I could.

I didn't do it like they do in the movies, holding the barrel and hitting with the butt. I hit him with the barrel and that was because I remembered a guy in a bar one time telling how he hit somebody on the head and the gun went off and he shot himself in the arm and even though it was only a flesh wound he would never do it that way again.

When I hit Billy Cigar, he dropped like a stone onto the floor of his office.

Quick as I could I dragged him inside and went to close the door, but there was a box on the floor that was in the way, so I pulled that inside too. And then I had a look at what I'd done.

I could see right away that Billy was bleeding. Someone else I might have put a bandage on his head, if I had one, but with Billy I wouldn't give him the satisfaction, so the first thing I did was go through his pockets and I found my own money along with the keys he took from me.

There was also a notebook and a pen and a cigar case and a couple of pieces of candy, and then I found Billy's wallet. I thought maybe I was going to be rich, but there was only six bucks in it. I've heard tell about how rich people walk around broke, but that's sure not the way I'd do it if I was rich.

Even though it was only six bucks, I put Billy's wallet and all the other stuff in my own pockets.

Then I thought it would be good to tie him up. I went around the room pulling the electric wires out of the lights and a clock and the TV and that gave me plenty to tie Billy's hands tight behind him. I also tied his ankles together, and his knees, and then his elbows behind his back, which was a thing I learned in the old days in Detroit, that the more a guy can't move, the less trouble he'll make.

And just then, someone knocked on the door.

I was crouched behind Billy's back and in that split moment I couldn't remember where I left the gun and I nearly fell over grabbing for it when I saw it on the floor.

A guy outside said, "Night, boss. I'm shoving off now."

I couldn't think what to do, so I said, "Yeah. Night." And then I got the gun in my two hands and aimed it at the door in case the guy came in.

But whoever it was said, "See you tomorrow," and went away, and I sat back down by Billy's body, and that was the very first time that I felt shaky about what I was doing. I just sat there for a while to calm down again.

That was when I realized that maybe Billy's own club wasn't the best place to wait for him to wake up to talk to, even though it was convenient because we were both already there. I began to think about other places to go when I also realized I hadn't looked in Billy's box, and so I pulled that over and opened it up and I found it was full of paper money. I counted more than four thousand dollars before I got to some checks at the bottom, and all that money was a pure bonus and all the better now that Miller and Fred were never going to pay me what they owed.

What I did then was close the box up and look at the watch on Billy's wrist, which said the time was after three in the morning.

I left Billy where he was in the office and I went out to get Barb's car.

40.

When I got back, Billy wasn't where I left him. For just a quick moment I got a flash of real anger at him because he ought to have known to stay where he was when he woke up, what with finding his arms and legs all tied. My intentions about him were clear from that even if I never said them out loud in so many words because he was unconscious.

But before I got to worrying about where he'd went, the telephone crashed on the floor and that was because Billy had rolled behind the desk and onto the phone wire where it came out of the wall. Right away I went over and dragged him back to the middle of the room and all the time I was saying, "*Bad* Billy. *Naughty* Billy."

Then, so he couldn't say I wasn't being fair by not telling him what I wanted, I went to his head end and I bent down so's he could see me, and I pointed the gun up his nose. I said, "Where is Barb?"

He was wide awake, but he didn't answer my question. Instead he said, "You're dead, you little fuck."

Well, that was pure rudeness and I hit him across his mouth with my gun barrel. And then I said something strange, which was, "You are about the most cussedest kid I ever did see, and that's a fact."

Those words just popped out of my mouth, though after I said them I knew where they came from, because my daddy said the very same words to me one time for messing my pants and he was ready to give up on me once and for all. That sure was what I was feeling now about Billy Cigar who wouldn't answer a simple question even though I asked him straight out.

I quit right there trying to reason with him. What I did was take his shoes off with the idea to stuff a sock in his mouth to make him quiet while I moved him. All the time I worked at his feet he kept on saying repulsive things, so it was a pure relief when I got the sock into his mouth and tied it tight in place with the wire out of the back of the telephone. Even then he had more to say, but I couldn't tell the words.

I dragged him down the corridor to the parking lot, which is where I had Barb's car backed up. But when I opened the trunk lid I saw my sleeping bag and accordion file, so I left Billy on the ground while I moved my own things to the passenger seat.

Only then, when I lifted Billy up to put him in the trunk, he went awkward and wouldn't bend his legs, so I had to smack his knees with the gun a couple of times to make him cooperate and finally I got him in.

Once I closed the lid on him I went back into the club. I picked up the cash box and brought it to the passenger seat in the car alongside my own things and then I drove out onto the street. The driving was easy as could be because I was calm now and getting used to Barb's car.

* * *

I drove to the Fairgrounds. At first I went in through the hole in the fence and scouted around, but there were no cars or people anywhere close. I could have dragged Billy in that way, but instead what I did was dig up my wire cutters and use them to cut the chain on the main gate. Once I had the gate open I drove straight past the guard's hut to the building where all the dogs were kept.

I backed the car up to the door where I got taken in that first time, but I went myself around the side and crawled in the bathroom window. I made my way to the room where I met Cobb and Pete and I turned the lights on as I went. A whole lot had happened since I was afraid Pete was going to kill me for my toes.

The dogs next door heard me through the wall and they started to bark. That gave me the impulse to take a look at them, but I didn't do it. When you're in the middle of business, you've got to keep your mind on the job and not let it wander, which is an important part of success.

Once all the lights were on I went out through the door and opened Barb's trunk. Billy didn't try to say anything through the sock and I wondered if maybe he was dead, but then he shook a little and started growling so I knew he wasn't.

Getting him out was a lot harder than putting him in, even though he wasn't fighting me, which was because of the awkward angle for lifting. I lost my grip and he dropped onto the road but I managed to move my foot out of the way in time. Then I dragged him inside by the legs.

The dogs next door started to barking again but even so it was quiet enough to talk so I pulled my gun out. I undid the wire around Billy's face, and I took the sock out of his mouth and I said, "Where's Barb?"

He didn't answer at first and he took a couple of deep breaths and licked around his lips and then he said, "This *can't* be about some two-bit whore."

I kicked him in his ribs, and I said, "Answer the question."

He said, "You'll beg me to kill you a hundred times before I let you die."

For sure Billy's attitude was all wrong for doing the business I wanted to do, so I fixed the sock back in his mouth. I put the gun up his nose and I thought about shooting one of the bullets so it grazed his head. But then I got a different idea, which was just as well because I hadn't ever shot a gun before and I might not get my aim right for just a graze and then I'd never find out where Barb was. Instead I went over to the table that had the microwave oven on it.

I lifted the oven onto the floor, and I pushed it up against the wall and made some space in front of it. Out the side of my eye I could see Billy twisting around so's he could keep track of what I was doing. I didn't mind that, but I kicked him a couple of times before I sat down, just to let him know I hadn't forgotten him.

What I did was play with the oven's buttons to find out how to make it work. And then I opened the door and tried the buttons again, but it wouldn't go on with the door open, so I looked around the room for a piece of baling wire or a coat hanger.

What I found was some stiff cardboard and a couple of bits of wood, and though it took me a while I managed to fill the latch hole and make the oven think the door was closed. That way I could turn the oven on and off even though the door was wide open.

Then I dragged Billy over to the microwave. He'd been watching me but just to make sure I held his head up and turned the oven on and off in front of his eyes. He understood, all right, because he tried to twist and roll. But the good tying-up job I'd done meant it was easy for me to stick his head inside the oven and keep it there by sitting on his chest like I was a jockey after all.

Once everything was set, I took the sock out of his mouth. He said, "Are you crazy?"

But I was happy about that because his voice was truly frightened for the very first time, so I knew we were finally ready to do business.

I turned the oven on.

"What are you doing, you little fuck?"

I said, "Tell me about Barb."

"Turn it off, for Christ's sake! Turn it off! I'll tell you anything you want!"

"Barb," I said.

"All right. All right. She came to the club and hung around all afternoon. I gave her a couple in the office but that wasn't enough for her and she said how bad she wanted us to go someplace private, so later on I took her out."

"Where?"

"You going to turn that thing off?"

"Where did you take Barb?"

"Soon as we got in the car she started honking about we had to go to her place, but I wasn't having any of that. I keep a place of my own, which is all equipped, and I sure as hell don't go anywhere that I haven't checked out. But, no, my place wouldn't do and the further we went the crazier she got and eventually she jumped out of the car."

"She what?"

"Opened the door while we were doing fucking forty miles an hour. C'mon! It's getting hot in here! Turn it off! And these things screw up your eyes, don't they?"

"Is Barb all right?"

"How do I know?"

"Didn't you stop?"

"Of course not. Wasn't anything to do with me. I didn't push her. She jumped."

"But you're supposed to stop when there's an accident."

"I can feel my hair shriveling! I can smell it burning!"

"Where is Barb now?"

"I don't know! I don't know!"

"You just left her on the street?"

"Yeah. No. I guess. I didn't stop. I don't know!"

"What street was it?"

"I don't know! Michigan Street. Way out West Michigan

Street. O.K.? Turn it off! Turn it off! My brain hurts. It's hot! I'm burning up in here!"

Suddenly, despite all the noise of Billy shouting and banging his head around trying to get it out of the oven, I heard someone at the door behind me. Billy heard it too because he called out, "Help! Help me! He's fucking killing me!"

I got my gun out of my pocket and because Billy was distracted I banged it on the oven a couple of times. "Where is Barb *now*?" I said.

"Help! Help! Help! Help!"

By then I had to turn to the door to see who it was. And standing there was Pete.

"Help!" Billy yelled. "He's cooking me to death!"

Pete came towards me. I pointed the gun straight at him but he didn't take the slightest notice. "What the hell is going on here, runt?"

"Help!"

I said, "Don't you come any closer. I'm finding out where Barb is," but Pete kept walking.

I was about to shoot when I remembered him saying what would happen to me if I ever crossed him. Before I could decide for sure whether shooting him counted as crossing him, he bent down and pushed the gun away.

"Get off the guy," Pete said.

"He hasn't told me where Barb is yet."

"Get *off*!" So I got off. Pete pulled the oven wire out of the wall and then he dragged Billy clear.

"Oh thank you, thank you!" Billy said and he was blubbering to beat the band and I could see his face was red like he had sunburn and his hair was kind of melted.

Pete turned to me. "Wait in my car."

"But Barb—"

"Get out of here!"

I left.

41.

But the door I went through took me into the dog room and right away the dogs set off howling. There were maybe twenty of them, in cages, and they were all hopping around and howling to be let out. It was one of the saddest sights I've ever seen.

I've spent my own time in a cage, and it was a place I hated more than anywhere in the whole world. It nearly drove me crazy. Seeing those dogs brought back my caged feeling and I couldn't help myself from going dog to dog pulling the doors wide open, every single one, and I set those dogs free.

They didn't need to be asked twice and they jumped out and in no time they were making more noise than ever. They ran around the room and barked and carried on and I felt like I had finally done something really good in my life.

I watched them till I got the idea that I should open the door to the outside, in case some of the dogs wanted to run away and be a stray, though it's not a life for everyone. But when I opened the dog room door I saw Pete's car and that reminded me of what I was supposed to be doing.

I got in Pete's car and waited. From there I could see some of the dogs find the open door and stick their noses out. And then a few of them came through and ran away even though they were only young and probably hadn't been outdoors alone before in their entire lives. Watching that happen made me feel proud. There wasn't anything I wanted so much as for those dogs who ran away to have good lives, and it wasn't only big ones that did it.

And then it came into my mind that I could run away too, if I wanted. I took ahold of the door handle, but I didn't do it. What I found was that, in my heart, I didn't want to run away, even though maybe from his being cooked Billy would die and Pete would lock me up in jail and throw away the key.

And then I realized I wasn't so different from my daddy after all. Daddy screwed his life up by killing that cop, even though he never meant to do it. And now here I was, calm as could be and sitting in Pete's car, and I didn't know for sure that I would have ever turned Billy's oven off, or that I wouldn't have pulled the trigger of the gun I pointed at Pete. Yet I'd never given a single thought to whether I was screwing up my life.

But you can be like your daddy and better at the same time. Because I also knew that I wasn't going to hide and try to get out of taking my medicine, which is what my daddy tried to do. If I lit out now I'd be letting Pete down. And I didn't want to do that because he trusted me.

Letting down someone's trust is a terrible feeling to feel, which I knew from my own experience because it was me that put my own daddy in jail.

Daddy came back to the house the night he killed the cop. He came in all wet, and right away us kids could tell he was scared. He said, "There's men a-gonna come to the door. Y'all gotta say I'm not here. Y'all got that?" And then Daddy went down in the basement, and we knew he was going to hide in the coal chute, because that's where he hid one time before, when some of his friends looked all over for him and they never found him.

Sure enough, before long there was pounding on the door and us kids just huddled together at the bottom of the stairs and we watched as the door shook and finally broke and a bunch of policemen came in. There seemed like about a hundred of them and they headed off to different parts of the house and they even had a big dog with them, and us kids, all of us, we started up to cry.

But there was this one cop, and he looked to be a giant, he was so big, and he came down the hall to where we were and we nearly shit ourselves, we were so scared. But then he kneeled down and I can still remember he had this soft warm voice, so quiet and kind that right away it made me miss my momma all over again, even though she'd been dead for two years and never hardly talked to me like that anyhow. And this cop said, "Don't you worry yourselves about all the noise, kids. I won't let anything bad happen to you," and then he reached out to hug us together. Wayne wouldn't let him, but me and Cissy got gathered up in this cop's big arms and right away I felt better.

And then the cop said, "Son, if you know where your daddy is, just you tell me, and everything will be all right."

He was the first cop I ever talked to and I believed him and I told him that Daddy was in the coal chute.

"What?"

"It's my fault, runt." Pete was getting in the car and he startled me so much I jumped away from him and banged off the door. He said, "I let you run on your own for too long. It was a mistake in judgment. The consequences are my responsibility, not yours."

I didn't know for sure what he meant, but it sounded like Billy was bad.

Pete said, "I've got to take Sigra to the hospital to see if there's anything they can do for him. After that we'll deal with you."

I said, "It was your idea!"

"What was?"

"Microwaving a puppy!"

He scratched at his beard. After a while he said, "Can you concentrate on reality long enough to drive somewhere?"

"I can drive," I said.

"Then get in that yellow car and follow me once I get Sigra into mine. When we get to the hospital, park on the street. I'll find you when I'm ready. Do you think you can manage that?"

While I was waiting in Barb's car I got the things on the passenger seat together. I rolled my accordion file, the gun and Billy's cash box into my sleeping bag. That made them all one thing to carry if I had to, or if they took it off me and put me in jail. Maybe they wouldn't look inside. That way when I got out at least I'd have the money in Billy's box to get me started again. No way would Miller and Fred be paying me my fifty thousand now, not if they could put me in jail instead. But this time I could use jail for making up songs and maybe when I got out I'd be ready to do my public access show. Especially if I had some money to be my own sponsor with.

Then Pete came out the door with Billy over his shoulder. He put Billy in his car on the back seat. Billy was untied, but he was all floppy and not helping.

42.

Pete drove to the hospital, which was the Methodist and it didn't take us long even going slow. Pete ran in and came back with guys in white coats and they pulled Billy out and put him on a trolley.

I moved Barb's car up the street and parked. I waited for a long time before Pete parked his car behind me. When I saw him coming I threw my sleeping bag onto the back seat and sure enough Pete got in and sat down next to me. "Top of the list," he said, "give me that goddamn gun."

Because it was in the sleeping bag I had to crawl into the back so I could find it without unrolling the whole thing. Meanwhile Pete said, "Makes me nervous as hell, sitting in a car with a crazy killer with a gun."

"Is Billy dead?"

"Not yet, no thanks to you."

"But is he going to die?"

"We're all going to die," Pete said. But then he said, "Sigra's got burns and a splitting headache. However, they managed to wake him up."

"That's good," I said.

"When I left he was telling everybody how bad he wants you dead."

"So he's going to be all right?"

"Too early to tell, but if you ask me, tonight at dinnertime his nose will fall off into his salad, and his brain will drip out on his steak like mushroom sauce."

"If he's hungry enough to eat, he's not that sick," I said, which was something my momma used to say.

"The doctor doesn't know. He's never seen a microwaved head before. He nearly wet himself, he's so excited. He'll be able to write the case up for a medical journal and get himself a better job. So you've done somebody a good turn, runt. And it does mean that Sigra will get every care and attention."

I said, "I hit Billy over the head back at the club. Maybe that's why he's got a headache."

"Jesus, runt, you're a menace to society."

"No I'm not!" I said.

I found the gun and gave it to him. Pete looked at it. He released the chamber. "Bullets too." Then he said, "There's a fucking spike in the barrel."

"Is there?"

"If you'd pulled the trigger and got one of these old bullets to fire, it would have blown your arm off."

"Oh."

"Where'd you get this thing?"

"I won it in a card game."

"Time to fold your hand, little fella." Pete put the bullets in one pocket and the gun in another. Then he said, "I told the doctor it was a domestic accident. He didn't believe me, but he didn't care."

"I've had an idea about Barb," I said.

"Who?" but then I could see he remembered.

"Billy said she jumped out of the car while it was moving, on West Michigan Street. So she's probably in the hospital somewhere herself. Could even be this one."

But instead of answering Pete looked at me and didn't talk, and it was like he had no intention in his mind to think about Barb at all. But I hadn't got this close to finding her that I was going to stop.

I said, "I'm not doing *anything* till I talk to Barb." And sat deep where I was in the back seat and I folded my hands across my chest.

Pete didn't speak for such a long time that I began to get frightened about what he might do, but finally what he did was get out of the car.

He said, "Are you coming or not?" and I followed and we walked back over to the hospital. Inside they phoned around and it turned out that Barb was in the hospital on the IU campus and I drove in Barb's car behind Pete driving in his own.

43.

The ward Barb was on wasn't intensive care, but even so the nurse wouldn't let us see her. He said, "Do you *know* what time it is? It's five forty-eight in the a.m."

Pete said, "I am a police officer. Your patient was with a man when she was injured. That man has suffered a savage attack tonight himself. We must talk to the young woman, now."

It didn't make much sense to me and maybe it didn't to the nurse either because he said, "You don't look like policemen."

"If you're going to check us out, be quick about it," Pete said, and all of a sudden he was the mean-as-hell Pete, only this time it wasn't aimed at me.

He gave the nurse a telephone number and said, "Ask anybody there to describe Lieutenant Leroy Powder." And at the same time Pete took my gun out of his pocket and started loading up the bullets again. He said, "We don't have much time. We've got decisions to make that are a matter of life and death."

The nurse couldn't take his eyes off Pete loading the gun. "Fuck it," he said. "I was about to wake them up for breakfast anyhow."

Half Barb's face was bandaged and one of her arms was in a cast. I left Pete by the door and walked over to her bedside. I shook her gently on a shoulder but she didn't want to wake up, because the first thing she said was, "Go away."

"Barb, it's Jan."

"Who?" and she tried to twist out from under my hand, but that started something inside her to hurting, and she moaned and lay back and said, "Oh Lord. Oh Lord."

"Jan Moro," I said. "I brought your car to the hospital so you don't have to fetch it from the Linger Longer when you get out of here. I'm putting the keys on the bedstand." I rattled the keys so she could hear. "The car's down in the parking lot whenever you need it."

"Let me be!" she said in a way that was almost crying and in a sharp moment it reminded me of how my momma talked sometimes in the bathtub not long before she died.

But I couldn't let Barb be like I let my momma, because for sure as soon as I left Barb's bed Pete would pack me off to jail because of what I did to Billy, no matter what he said about it being his responsibility.

I said, "Barb, I've *got* to tell you about Billy and Ramón. Then I'll go."

She didn't say anything; but even though her eyes were closed I knew she was listening and awake. I said, "You already found out for yourself what an evil dangerous guy Billy is, but what I still have to tell you is how I saw Ramón tonight, at your house."

She moved to sit up, only it hurt. She said, "You saw Ramón?"

"I went inside your house to see if you were there, but then

Ramón came into the bedroom and caught me by surprise. And, Barb, he had a gun out and he thought I was Billy and he was going to shoot me, he really was, only I wasn't Billy, so he didn't do it."

I thought she might say something to that, or be surprised, but she didn't and she wasn't so I said, "Barb, did you hear? He was going to shoot Billy like a dog and go back to his own country and try to be a hero."

I thought that was the whole warning I had to say but suddenly I said, "Barb, if you'd been in your bedroom with Billy, Ramón would have shot you at the same time, just for being there. He already thought maybe Billy killed you and he didn't care less if you were alive or dead. Ramón is a bad man, Barb, and so is Billy and you shouldn't ought to have anything to do with either one of them."

In a little voice Barb said, "Does Ramón know where to find me?"

"No. You're safe in here."

She said, "I did everything I was supposed to. And more. It's not my fault. I tried. I couldn't have tried any harder."

She rested for a moment and I didn't say anything back and then she said, "Billy was going to hurt me. I was in his car and he talked about what he was going do to me and what he was going to do it with. Even if I'd gone where he wanted there was no way I could have gotten him back to the house, no way at all. But make Ramón pay me anyhow, will you? Make him pay me the full amount, because I did everything I could. Nobody could have done any better."

When we left I could tell that Pete thought Barb was hard and that she should have known better than to get mixed up with Ramón and Billy and that she didn't deserve any sympathy. And I could see how he might think that way.

But he didn't understand Barb like I did. Barb had told me stories about her life and then she let me stay overnight at her house. Her seeming hard now wasn't her real self. It was only like how my momma was when she got sick, and that's just the time that folks need to have extra understanding.

At first Momma would let me pour her medicine into a spoon, and later on into her glass, but when she got sicker, Momma drank the medicine straight from the bottle and there was nothing she'd let me do to help her. When I asked she snapped my head off. That's how you get when you're sick, and it makes you seem hard, even when you're not underneath.

Still, all you can do is try to be a help. I'd warned Barb about Billy and Ramón now, but I couldn't make her not work for them if she still wanted to. Though maybe Billy would die and then there would be no job for Barb and at least that side would all have worked out for the best.

"What?"

We were sitting in Pete's car. He said, "I didn't see López Oso at her house."

"How could you? You weren't there. You were meeting with Miller and Fred."

"Runt, I've been on your tail all night long."

I didn't understand what he meant.

Pete said, "You never stay put when you're supposed to, so I met Miller and Feske outside your motel. We laughed our heads off when you came out of your room."

"You followed me?"

"I kept giving you rope, runt. But I let it go too long. I got it wrong, so everything that happened was my fault."

"Does that mean I'm not going to jail?"

"I don't think putting you in jail would help anybody," Pete said. "I think it would be a lot better all around if I just kill you instead."

44.

At the bus station we went into the Burger King and Pete bought me about everything there was for breakfast on the menu. "The condemned man ate a hearty meal," he said.

I carried the tray over to a table but instead of sitting down Pete said, "I'm going to call Carollee."

"Will she be up?"

"She will after I call her," he said. He took a couple of steps towards the concourse, which is where the phones are, but then he came back. "You'll stay here, won't you, runt?"

"Yeah," I said. "Of course. Where would I go?"

I started with the French toast sticks and I put lots of butter on and I dipped them into the syrup. They tasted wonderful. There is nothing in this world for making food taste good like being hungry.

When I finished all the toast I started on the eggs and the bacon and the sausages. But then the coffee was cool. I thought about taking it back, since it was paid for, but I didn't want Pete to find the table empty.

And then I thought it was funny that you cook stuff like toast and sausage and bacon and eggs when you want them, but you make coffee way ahead of time and then you have to keep it hot. You'd have thought in this day and age there'd be something you could put in coffee that would give off its own heat when you added water. That way you wouldn't have to make the coffee till you wanted it.

The more I thought about self-heating coffee, the more it seemed like the kind of idea that could make me rich, if I found the right guy to put it to and the right way to put it to him.

"What?"

Pete was sitting across from me. "Are you all right?"

"Sure."

"If you say so." Then he said, "Carollee will see to it that Missing Persons in Chicago takes you to Rosie. We'll also use them to get some money to you."

"How much?" I said.

He rubbed his beard with both his hands. "You're going to have to trust me on that."

It was a time to row with the current, so I said, "O.K." And besides, Pete bought me a Chicago ticket before we went for breakfast so I already had what I wanted most.

But then Pete took out his own wallet and he gave me all the paper money left in it which was over seventy dollars. He said, "There'll be more in Chicago by tomorrow."

"Thanks," I said and I put Pete's money in my pocket.

That's when I remembered the other things already in my pocket, Billy's wallet and his notebook and his pen and his candy and the papers off his desk. I put them all on the table in front of Pete. I said, "When you kill me, you can tell Billy you found this stuff on my corpse."

"What the fuck is it?" he said.

"When I was at the club I took it out of Billy's pockets and off his desk."

"All this is Sigra's?" He picked up the wallet and looked in it. "Six bucks?"

"That's all there was."

I went back to eating while Pete looked through Billy's things. He spent the most time on Billy's notebook and went through every page.

When I was wiping off my mouth for about the last time, Pete said, "Do you know what this *is*?" And then he said, "No, of course you don't." But I could tell he liked it. He said, "Runt, you may not have to be dead for so long after all."

I said, "When it's in the newspapers about my body being found, will you cut it out for me so I can show it to Rosie?"

They called Chicago over the PA and Pete walked me all the way to the bus. It was only about a quarter full and I found a window seat where I could see Pete standing and waiting for me to leave. What I did to settle was unroll my sleeping bag because I was tired and I had it in my mind to sleep the whole way to Chicago. It was already warm on the bus and the sleeping bag would give me someplace soft to put my head.

But by unrolling the bag I found my accordion file and Billy's cash box and that started me to thinking. Pete's plan, if Billy got well, was to say he'd gone and killed me because Billy was so mad at what I'd done. And it would say all about my body being found dead in the newspapers. What with Pete already having saved Billy's life by pulling me off when his head was in the microwave, Pete would become Billy's big buddy and it wouldn't take him long to get whatever he needed to put Billy in jail with, which was how long I had to stay dead in Chicago.

But what I realized on the bus was that when Pete gave Billy back his wallet and the other stuff, Billy was going to ask about the cash box. And Pete would say, "What cash box?" And then Billy would think that Pete had kept the four thousand bucks for himself. And chances were that would make Billy mad with Pete and not think of him as a buddy after all.

Billy was a dangerous guy to have mad at you and he could even go as far as killing Pete which would be the end of the plan and not nice for Pete and I'd have to stay dead forever.

"What?"

But it was only the driver starting the engine.

I put off the hard decision another second, but then I got up and I said, "Hey, wait a minute," and I got off the bus.

Pete was still there. He said, "You *are* going to Chicago, runt. You are *not* changing your mind."

"Of course," I said. "But I was just thinking."

"What about?"

"That it would be a real good idea if you didn't give Billy back his stuff."

"Why not?"

"To tell the truth, when I took Billy's wallet there was a lot of money in it. So if you give it back with just six bucks, you're going to get in trouble. It'll be better if you just say you didn't find any of the things I took when you killed me."

You'd have thought Pete would've thanked me, but he didn't. He looked at me but he didn't say a thing.

With the bus engine already running, I couldn't stay around waiting for him to be polite. I said, "I better get back on now," which is what I did and when it started to move I waved Pete goodbye.

I couldn't make him do what I said, but at least I tried to help keep him out of trouble. That was the least I could do after he bought my Chicago ticket and gave me his last paper money. I never like to tell an untrue story to somebody, but there are times it's for the best.